Merry Murders

A Sanford 3rd Age

David W Robinson

in association with Ocelot Press

Ocelot Press

© David W Robinson 2024
All right reserved

Edited by Maureen Vincent-Northam
Cover Design Rhys Vincent-Northam

No part of this book may be used or reproduced in any manner whatsoever without written permission of the author except for brief quotations used for promotion or in reviews. This is a work of fiction. Names, characters, and incidents are used fictitiously.

First published by Darkstroke Books 2019

Chapter One

'I have fifty... I'm looking for fifty-five... fifty-five I'm looking for...'

For Terry Bailey, half the fun of property auctions was watching the twists and turns of Archie Hepple's rubbery features, most noticeable when the bids were not flooding in. Archie was about sixty years old, and had inherited the auction house from his father about twenty years back, a time when there was a surfeit of goods for auction. These days, a town like Sanford did not enjoy much in the way of antiques or other high-value items, and most of Archie's business was repossessions or lost property auctions, and especially real property; houses, shops, small factories, the kind of property that was not lost.

Archie put on a pained expression. 'I'll take three. So I'm looking for fifty-three. Come on, you builders. Fifty-three for a piece of prime prop like this. Do I have fifty-three?'

'The only time I've seen a face like that is when my business partner hasn't hit the smallest room for three days,' Terry whispered to the man alongside him.

'Are you bidding, Mr Bailey?' Archie demanded.

'No. Sorry, Arch'. I was just saying—'

Archie had lost interest already. 'I'll take two. Come on. I'm asking for fifty-two. You know it's worth it and you know that somewhere along the

1

line one of you will bottle out and make the next bid. Come on, give me fifty-two.'

The auction room was barely half-full, and most of the bidders were like Terry and his partner, Denny Dixon: pros. Builders and small-time developers who wanted the terraced house at number seventeen Kimbolton Terrace, but were not willing to pay over the odds for it.

Stood to one side of her father and looking in Terry's direction, was Ros Hepple. Ros and Tel had been in a half-hearted relationship long enough for him to know that the promises she was making with her baby blue eyes often came with conditions, such as: "I will honour my promise if you can see your way clear to making the next bid."

It was tempting, but unfortunately, she (and Tel) were up against the reaction of Denny Dixon to Tel making the next bid. Denny was not only Tel's business partner but also his brother-in-law, and a self-confessed expert on auctions. Before they arrived at the auction room, he made it clear that they would not enter the bidding until it got fifty-eight/fifty-nine, by which time most of the suckers would be cleared out.

But Archie was struggling to find any further bidders, and there was the danger that this house would go for an even fifty thousand, and to an undeserving amateur at that.

Tel was in a quandary. Who was he most keen to please? His brother-in-law or his part time girlfriend? Ros could be fierce when she didn't get her own way, and although Denny would snap and snarl, he was easier to handle, if only because Tel was bigger than him and he was married to Tel's sister... mainly because he was married to Tel's sister.

Consequently, when Archie hit the desperation line and declared, 'I'm going up in ones. I have fifty, I'm looking for fifty-one,' Tel gave Ros the nod, and she nudged Archie who aimed the stem of his gavel and said, 'I have fifty-one. Thank you, Terry Bailey. I'm on fifty-one, who'll give me fifty-two?'

At the mention of Tel's full name, Denny looked up into his eyes, but in contrast to Ros, his partner's gaze was not overflowing with the milk of human kindness; more the blood and venom of murderous intent.

'I thought I told you—'

As he spoke, Denny jabbed his index finger into Tel's chest, and Archie took full advantage of the gesture.

'I have fifty-two with Mr Dennis Dixon.'

Denny dropped his hands to his side, faced the podium, and glared murder at Archie. 'That wasn't a bid, Mr Hepple.'

'Your normal method of bidding, Mr Dixon, is to raise your index finger.'

'Yes, but not to jab it in Tel's rib cage.'

'I don't know how I'm supposed to know the difference,' Archie observed with a smirk which told everyone in the room that he knew the difference all right. Before Denny could object further, the auctioneer opened the bidding to the rest of the room. 'I have fifty-two. Do I hear fifty-three?'

He received an instant bid from Ian Parsloe, one of Tel and Denny's great rivals. 'I have fifty-three... fifty-four, fifty-five, fifty-six, fifty-seven... The bid is against you, Messrs Dixon and Bailey. Do I hear fifty-eight? I'm selling once at fifty-seven. I'll take a half. Second time at fifty-seven. Come on, all you builders, this is a snip. You'll double your money in a month. I'll take fifty-seven, five. Selling for the third and final time at fifty-seven.'

Archie was about to bring the gavel down when Denny reluctantly raised his finger, and another round of bidding began.

According to Tel's calculations, he and his brother-in-law had had more aggravation from Parsloe than any other small building contractor in Sanford, and Tel was well aware that it would needle Denny if Parsloe were to win the bid, and Archie always loved it when Denny and Parsloe slugged it out toe to toe.

Prior to the auction, Dennis insisted they didn't want to pay any more than £65,000, but Parsloe was unwilling to let go and Archie revelled in the prospect of his two percent commission.

Tel was strongly tempted to intervene and counterbid, but he knew better. He had worked with Denny long enough to know when to keep his mouth shut, otherwise they could end up bidding against each other.

As the price moved on to sixty-six, a fresh bid came in from the rear of the room. It was from a woman, but she was so small that neither Tel,

Denny, nor Parsloe could see her. Parsloe countered with a tentative bid of sixty-six and a half, and the woman's paddle showed above the crowd, adding five hundred pounds to the price. After a few more bids, Parsloe had had enough. Denny hedged for a moment under Archie Hepple's greedy eye, but decided that the property was simply not worth it and shook his head. Hepple finally brought the gavel down on £71,500.

'Sold to paddle number seventy-eight.'

Parsloe pointed a threatening finger at Denny, and over the general hum of conversation, warned, 'I'll beat you yet, Dixon.'

Irritated at having been beaten by a third-party, Denny retorted, 'Any time you think you're big enough.' The comment was lost in the background noise, and Parsloe turned away, skulking out of the auction room.

Denny turned his irritation on his partner. 'I blame you for that, Tel. I've told you before, leave the bidding to me.'

'Yeah well it wasn't me who outbid you and pimple brain Parsloe, was it?'

'No, but if you hadn't started bidding when you did, we might have got it before she started. It's your fault.'

'You always say that, Denny. It doesn't matter what goes wrong, it's always my fault. You even blamed me when that pilot took us to Fuerteventura.'

'Yes well—'

'It wasn't my fault that Lanzarote airport was shut.'

'Who booked the holiday?' Denny demanded.

'Me. But—'

'There you are then. Come on. Let's see if we can get this mystery bidder to sell to us for a small profit.'

While Archie began pitching the next property, promising prospective buyers, developers, and demolition teams that this was a once-in-a-lifetime opportunity, the two men made their way to the back room of the auction house, where Archie's wife, Frankie, a woman never seen in the auction room during a sale, would be sorting out the paperwork with the new owner of seventeen Kimbolton Terrace.

Archie and Frankie always worked this way. It saved clogging up the sale room with people who had already bought, and really wanted to pick up their keys and get away to their new investments, rather than hang about until the end of the auction which could be anything up to two or three hours hence. Once the gavel came down on any lot, the buyer retired to the back room where Frankie would have the paperwork ready for processing, and the keys for handing over.

A busty, flame-haired temptress in her late fifties, Denny had long ago decided that in her younger days, she would have been a spectacularly good looking woman, and Tel agreed but with some reservations.

'Not my type at all. Not keen on redheads. Too bad-tempered.'

The comment was odd because Tel, like his sister, was red-haired and had the legendary temper to match.

'And she must have been round the block a time or two,' Tel went on. 'I meanersay, Ros don't look a bit like her, so who was the father?'

'She's not Ros's real mother, you dipstick. Ros was from Archie's first wife. Her what left him.'

'Oh. Right. So who did she leave him for?'

'An estate agent.'

'Ah. He must be Ros' dad then.'

Denny's malleable features queried his partner's intelligence. 'You're the one dating Ros. You should know all this.'

'We don't have time to talk about families.'

'I'll bet you don't.'

On entering the back room, they were absolutely astonished to learn that the buyer was none other than Vanessa Dixon, née Bailey, Denny's wife and Tel's older sister.

The Bailey family had lived next door to the Dixons for over forty years, as a result of which the firstborn to each family, Vanessa and Denny were all but brought up together. Tel came along two years later, and from there he and Denny became best friends, even though Denny left school before his then girlfriend's, now wife's, younger brother. Tel always insisted that the main reason behind Denny's chumminess was that, even though Tel was younger, he was always bigger and tougher and Denny had an unhappy habit of getting into trouble at school.

Not only at school…

And yet for all the times the younger Bailey

had saved his hide, he still had more feelings for the sister than his business partner, and eventually, they decided to get married. According to Denny, they had a strong marriage built on a solid foundation of love, trust, and mutual respect, and if you pushed her on the subject, Vanessa would agree with him, although privately she had been known to say that Denny was the best kind of husband – one who did as he was told.

On seeing his wife ready to sign the contracts, Denny's face dropped. 'Aw, Van, don't tell me you've just bought Kimbotlton.'

His wife swept a stray red hair out of her eyes, scribbled her signature on the contract, and demanded. 'Where else?'

'You were bidding against me and Tel.'

'I didn't know that, did I? I'm too small to see past all those big builders.' She dropped the pen on the contract and turned on the two men. 'You told me that you wanted to stop Parsloe at all costs, and I thought he was doing the bidding.'

'He dropped out at sixty nine and a half,' Tel reported.

'And I called it a day when you hit seventy one and half,' Denny complained. 'And thanks to you, we've just paid six grand over the top for it.'

It was not the wisest thing he could have said, as the gleam in his wife's eyes told him he would be sleeping on the settee for the next few nights.

'*Un fait accompli*,' Frankie said in perfect French augmented with a broad grin.

'A fate worse than death if you ask me,' Denny grumbled.

Tel elected to keep his distance from the argument, and stood back as an interested spectator.

'Those properties are selling for upwards of a hundred and twenty,' Vanessa insisted. 'You'll still pull a good pre-tax profit on it.'

Denny pulled a face. 'You haven't seen the amount of work that needs doing.'

'Then you'd better get on with it, hadn't you?'

Now the worry lines creased Tel's forehead. 'What about Joe Murray?' He took his sister's puzzled looked as a cue and went on, 'We're a bit behind on Tandy Street, and you know what Joe's like.'

Denny agreed. 'He's the size of a wet dishcloth.'

'And he has a bite like a Rottweiler with haemorrhoids,' Tel retorted.

Denny was more confident. 'Leave Joe Murray to me. I'll square it with him.'

Chapter Two

'Again?'

Having just heard the news that Sheila Riley was unwell for what had to be the sixth time since her return from honeymoon, Joe Murray's irritable features twisted into a veneer of anguish-cum-disbelief-cum-rage, and Brenda Jump could only respond with a shrug of her winsome shoulders, and only then when she had hung her coat in a locker at the rear of the kitchen.

Joe, stood by the open rear door, puffed on his cigarette, and vented his spleen. 'How many times is this, now? She's been like it ever since she came back from Cape Verde.'

Brenda switched on the kettle and prepared herself a beaker of tea. 'She can't help it, Joe, and she can't work while she's like that. The last thing any café needs is a member of staff with tummy trouble, especially if it's contagious.'

Joe's giant nephew, Lee, sneezed almost on cue, bringing a further round of remonstration from his uncle.

Lee wiped his runny nose. 'If you have to sneeze, lad, get out here. Don't be spreading your germs all over the bacon.' He took another bad-tempered drag on his cigarette, and flicked it out into the dark, December morning. 'I'd better phone your Cheryl.'

'Want me to do it, Uncle Joe? Only she's not well either, but I can get that mate of hers, Pauline, and her sister, Kayleigh to come in.'

Joe nodded and came away from the rear door, closing it to keep out the cold of an icy, rainy morning. While Lee was busy on the telephone, Joe manned the grill and hotplate, where the bacon, sausage, and other breakfast items were cooking in preparation for the morning rush.

A check on the time revealed that it was a little after half past six, and so far, The Lazy Luncheonette had seen just one customer, a passing trucker, who stopped to collect breakfast on a bun, which he took back out to his truck, and drove away.

For as long as Joe could remember (getting on for half a century) the café had opened at six, and the first hour was concerned largely with preparation. Chaos would follow. The draymen of Sanford Brewery would begin to turn up from seven fifteen onwards, and they would fill the dining area. At eight o'clock, one of the apprentices from Broadbent Autos, a large car repair works across the dual carriageway from the café, would arrive with their orders, Ingleton Engineering, would phone their order through just before nine o'clock, after which the clerical staff of the offices above and around the café would appear, all of them crying for a feed or at the very least, a cup of coffee to go, and it would be ten o'clock before things settled down. Even then, the impasse would be short lived. With just seven days to Christmas, Sanford Retail Park, a large shopping complex to the rear of the café, was at its busiest, and many of the shoppers walked across to

The Lazy Luncheonette, preferring the freshly cooked food to the often-tasteless and expensive varieties from the outlets inside the mall.

As the proprietor, Joe never claimed that Christmas was the busiest time of year. It would be an exaggeration. The Lazy Luncheonette's trade was consistent. As a sop to the Yuletide season, he carried extra stock in the shape of mince pies, Christmas cake, individual trifles, and such, but unlike the town centre shops, the number of customers did not vary more than a couple of percentage points.

Even so, the absence of a crew member placed extra work on him, Brenda and Lee, and although Pauline Watson, a woman who had worked for Joe casually on and off for a number of years, knew the ropes, she could not compare to the missing Sheila Riley.

Keeping one eye on the grills and hotplate, while making ready the large, metal teapot, which he used for serving customers, Joe complained again. 'This must be half a dozen times she's chucked sick. And has her doctor not sorted the problem?'

Lee put the phone down having arranged for Pauline to come in, and Brenda joined him at the cooking appliances. She spoke up in defence of her best friend. 'He takes samples, Joe, sends them off for analysis, and they've come back with all sorts of results, but nothing significant, nothing out of the ordinary, and as quickly as she gets right, she goes again.' Her brow knitted with deep-felt concern for her friend. 'I'm worried about it, I don't mind telling you. I think there's something deeper, something more serious going on, and they're just not getting to the bottom of it.'

'And what does Martin have to say about it?'

'He's sick with worry, too, but like all men, he's as much use as a chocolate fireguard.' Gently stirring a large pan of baked beans, she grumbled, 'Why is it men are so useless?'

'It's because we have more to worry about,' Joe retorted. 'Like trying to run a business.' He shifted his attention to his nephew. 'Lee, would you mind staying behind and helping with the cleaning this afternoon?'

Lee sniffed again, and ran a tissue over his nose. 'Course not, Uncle Joe. You always said that one day all this will be yours.'

Joe frowned. 'It's already mine. I said it will be yours.'

Lee nodded. 'That's what I just said.'

'Yeah, but… Forget it. I don't have time for your complicated thinking at this time of day.'

The first of the draymen arrived a little after seven o'clock; earlier than usual, but pleading pressure due to extra work stocking up pubs, clubs and supermarkets in the final rush up to Christmas. From then, was all hands to the pumps, Joe behind the counter, taking orders, serving tea, taking the cash, Brenda helping Lee, and when she had time to spare, assisting Pauline in delivering meals, and none of them had time to think about Sheila.

Outside, as the rush-hour gained momentum and traffic lost speed, Doncaster Road ground to its usual, early-morning halt (thanks to two sets of traffic lights within a hundred yards of each other). Rain, flecked with occasional spots of sleet, doused the windows and pavements and another frenetic two and a half hours was under way at Sanford's favourite eatery (according to Joe).

Martin Naylor, Sheila's new husband, rang at eight thirty as he arrived at Sanford Park Comprehensive, where he taught English Language, Literature and Drama, to tell them that she would be off sick until at least the New Year. Although Joe kept the conversation brief, he commiserated, asked Martin to give Sheila their regards, and then took it out on his customers. It was as water off a duck's back. Joe's irritability, which often spilled over into plain rudeness, was legendary throughout the town, and everyone had learned to ignore it.

Or better still, return it.

'Hey up, Joe,' said a singularly jovial drayman when he got to the front of the queue a little after a quarter to eight. 'Is it true you're playing the opposite of Santa Claus this year? Anti-Claus? You're gonna visit all the kids and nick the presents.'

'And the sherry and mince pie,' his mate chimed in with a large grin.

'Take the words off and clear and rearrange them into a well-known phrase or saying,' Joe retorted. 'Now stop clowning around and tell me what you want.'

'Full breakfast, two of, tea, two of, and a tenner out of the till.'

'No problem. That'll be forty-seven pounds

fifty to you.' Joe gave them a savage smile. 'Just getting into the part of Anti-Claus.'

To accommodate the (supposedly) more discerning customers from the offices above them, and some of those who came from the retail park, Joe had installed a three-cup barista coffee machine. At somewhere over three thousand pounds, the price almost gave him a coronary, but his negotiating skills managed to get five hundred off the total, and to be fair, it was a sound investment. The clerks, junior accountants, trainee legal executives and salespeople from the floors above them, craved their lattes, cappuccinos, mochas, and as word spread, it brought in more custom. It also gave Joe more opportunity to vent his irritation when someone asked for "expresso".

'It's espresso, you ignorant sod,' was his usual response.

When he drank coffee at all, Joe preferred instant, and he had no idea how the machine worked or how to operate it. Under the guidance of the fitter who installed it, Sheila had quickly learned the basics of both machine and ingredients, and without her, it fell upon Brenda. She was efficient, but lacked her friend's talent for latte art, and many of the customers were disappointed when their tulip looked more like a weed stalk, or their heart appeared as a blob. It prompted most to ask after Sheila's health.

The queries were welcome and by the time they came to settle at table five, where they took their morning break, it was the main topic of conversation and concern.

With Lee in the kitchen preparing lunches, and Pauline, texting on her smartphone, sat alongside Brenda, Joe worked on the cryptic crossword in the *Daily Express*, and Brenda rang Sheila. Only half listening to the one side of the conversation he could hear, Joe inked *warlock* into 9 across, *"See the law rock at Wells' timely vision (7)"*, and as Brenda ended the call, he concentrated on her.

'She's in a terrible state. She's running to the toilet every two minutes, and she can't keep anything down.'

'Her GP?'

'He sent samples for analysis… again. But Sheila's not hopeful of a result. It's all a huge puzzle, Joe, but she did tell me that Howard called to see her yesterday, and he was going to approach her GP this morning. Now whether…'

She trailed off as the café door open, and Howard Riley stepped in.

Brenda smiled a warm greeting. 'Well, talk of the devil.' She left her seat, moved behind the counter and prepared a cup of tea for Howard, who removed his topcoat, and took the seat alongside Joe.

A detective inspector, formerly with the Cambridgeshire police, he had transferred to Leeds after settling into a relationship with Joe's niece, DI Gemma Craddock, of Sanford CID. Tall, square-shouldered, with an athletic frame, he combined the necessary physical attributes of the modern police officer with the over-arching intelligence of a top class graduate, and an in-depth insight into criminal motives and activity.

After the Squires Lodge affair, Joe had arranged to buy the terraced house which had belonged to Howard's mother (one of the victims in the Squires Lodge scandal) but ownership of the property took a long time to settle, and it was only recently that they had exchanged contracts. From there, Joe had engaged a couple of builders to resurrect the interior, and in the meantime, he rented a council flat on Leeds Road.

Joe liked Howard. Without patronising, he was good to Gemma, and took a genuine interest not only in her but her friends and family.

His concern now, as he made clear when Brenda re-joined them, was his Aunt Sheila.

'I've spoken to Doctor Khalil, her GP, and he was a little more candid with me than he has been with her. He believes the entire business is psychosomatic.'

'How come he spoke to you?' Brenda asked. 'I mean patient confidentiality.'

'Simple enough. I stressed my family relationship to him and asked him purely for an overview nothing too private.' He smiled. ' It probably helped that I told him I'm a CID officer.

Suspending his interest in the crossword, Joe disagreed. 'Your Aunt Sheila is one of the most level-headed women I've ever met. I know she suffered when Peter passed away, but who wouldn't? They'd been married since forever. But she's had plenty of time to get over that, so how does Khalil get off with claiming it's all in her head?'

Howard drank some tea. 'I needed that.' He put the beaker back on the table and paused for a moment, formulating his thoughts. 'She was absolutely dedicated to Peter's memory. I think we all knew that. Then, last Christmas, she met Martin, and she fell in, er, fell in love for the second time.'

Brenda tutted. 'There's no need to be so coy about it, Howard. People of our age are permitted to fall in love, you know. It's not restricted to you young 'uns.'

Howard chuckled. 'I suppose so. It's just, er, strange talking about one's aunt falling in love.'

'Can we leave the Mills and Boon stuff out?' Joe grumbled. 'What does all this have to do with Sheila's state of mind?'

'It's complicated.'

Joe frowned upon Howard. 'So what am I? Thick as a brick? I can handle complicated. Get on with it.'

'Khalil believes that deep down, Sheila feels she's betraying her first husband's memory. But that sets up a conflict in her mind, because she really is in love with Martin. Most people suffer from such internal conflicts, and find them easy to rationalise. At the very worst, they'll produce fits of anger. In Sheila's case, these are deep-seated concerns, and to be fair, she can't really discuss them with Martin so early into their marriage. From his point of view, it might instigate a concern that he's second best and their marriage is one of convenience. In other words, she doesn't really love him as much as she did Peter, and she married him purely to give her a little support and companionship as she approaches her later years. Keeping it bottled up, keeping it hidden from him precludes episodes of open anger, so it's manifesting in these constant stomach complaints, all of which are genuine, physical illnesses, but which have a psychosomatic cause.'

His detailed explanation was greeted with silence. Beyond the counter they could hear Lee busy in the kitchen, and Pauline, having finished her break, lending him a hand, while outside on Doncaster Road, the rush-hour was over, but the sleet and rain appeared to have gathered momentum, and from the television came the distant sound of inconsequential morning magazine programmes.

Joe was the first to speak. 'I've never heard so much rubbish in my life.'

Brenda disagreed. 'It sounds reasonable to me. When we were waiting for you two to get back from Whitby on her wedding day, she was in a hell of a state. She said, and I quote, 'do you think it's a sign from Peter telling me not to remarry?' Joe, we both know how dedicated she was to Peter, and I don't think there's much doubt about her feelings for Martin. Marrying again is a massive upheaval in her life. That doesn't make it wrong, but it must mean huge changes.'

'Correct,' Howard declared. 'You've been to the bungalow many times, Joe. You must have noticed that almost every photograph was of Peter, or Peter and the boys, or the entire family. One of the first things she did when she agreed to marry

Martin was move those photographs. It's an enormous wrench, but as Brenda's just pointed out, that doesn't mean it's wrong.'

Joe went on the defensive. 'It's not that I'm not aware of all that, but I'm thinking in terms of Sheila as a person. She's smarter than Brenda and me put together, but she can be a snapper, and she's never had a problem speaking out, telling us exactly what's on her mind.'

'Yes, but she's not in love with you.'

Joe scowled at Brenda's comment. 'Thank the Lord for small mercies.' Before Brenda could come back at him, he threw another query at Howard. 'Has the doctor discussed this with Martin?'

'Yes. But Martin is a little reluctant to broach the matter with Sheila.'

Joe shook his head sadly. 'Whatever happened to plain speaking? You know, most of the world's problems could be solved if people stopped worrying about treading on one another's toes and began telling it like it is.'

'Thank you, the Secretary-General of the United Nations.' Brenda concentrated her annoyance on Joe. 'When we were in Cornwall you said I would get all the gory details when they came back from Boa Vista, and you were wrong. Sheila's told me next to nothing of their honeymoon, except that she enjoyed it – as far as she could, considering her tummy troubles – but she did tell me one thing which on reflection could be significant. They met at a Christmas party last year, and between then and now, there hasn't been a cross word between them. Martin wouldn't want to start the first argument.'

Joe deliberately shifted the subject sideways. 'Can we go to see her?' he asked of Howard.

'As far as I'm aware, yes. She's not contagious... at least, not according to Doctor Khalil she isn't, and I'm sure she'd be glad to see you both.' He focused on Brenda. 'Especially you.'

Joe pursed his lips. 'Wednesday. Things'll die off pretty quickly after lunch. Fancy nipping over there to see her?'

Brenda smiled broadly. She had been waiting for Joe to suggest it. 'You lead, I'll follow.'

Howard spent a further twenty minutes with them, assuring Joe that everything was fine with Gemma, although the pair did not see as much of each other as they would like.

'She works Sanford, I work North Leeds, and you know what police work is like, Joe. The scrotes don't take time off for Christmas.'

When Howard left, Joe folded away his newspaper, the crossword only half finished, and was preparing to move back behind the counter, to allow Lee his breaks, when the door opened and a familiar figure walked in.

It was almost impossible not to recognise Denny Dixon. In his mid to late thirties, a few inches taller than Joe, with a head of dark, curly hair, he was a stocky, muscular man, but his chronic sweet tooth had left him with a waistline almost as broad as his shoulders. He was also many weeks behind in the refurbishment of twenty-three Tandy Street, the house Joe had finally bought from Howard.

Denny's bulk did not deter Joe. He had vented his irritation on bigger men.

'I don't know where you get the brass nerve to come in here, Dixon. When the hell am I gonna move into Tandy Street?'

Denny surrendered with raised hands. 'Guilty, Joe. But we've had some problems.'

'Don't tell me. You're waiting for a skip.'

Denny tittered. 'Hee-hee. Haven't used that old chestnut for years. No, mate, I'm waiting for a gas engineer to commission the central heating, and a leccy to certify the rewiring.'

Lee emerged from the kitchen carrying a cup of tea and a sandwich. 'Hey up, Denny. Haven't seen you in yonks. Before I forget, Merry Bimbo.'

As Lee moved to a free table, Denny gave him a curious glance, which he then transferred to Joe.

'He means Merry Crimbo.'

'Oh.' Denny was still mystified. 'He says some queer things, your Lee.'

'Yes, well, he can't help being thick, can he?' Joe said it loud enough for Lee to hear. 'But you can help dithering about with my house. When am I gonna move in?'

'Ah, now, that's the thing, Joe. That's why I'm here. I've got serious problems now.'

'You'll have even more serious problems if I set Lee onto you. Stop—'

'Tel's been arrested.'

Denny's announcement did nothing to appease Joe's anger. 'Fighting? Again? I suppose he was drunk, was he?'

'No, no. Nowt like that. The filth have him walled up in Sanford nick. They're charging him with murder.'

Chapter Three

Joe greeted the announcement on several levels: elation (something he might be able to get his teeth into) annoyance (he had known Terry Bailey for years, and although he was a known scrapper, he always knew when to draw the line) and surprise (his niece, Gemma, would never hold anyone without solid evidence).

Brenda automatically brought a cup of tea to the table, and Denny drank gratefully.

'Tell me exactly what happened,' Joe ordered.

'We've just bought a new prop. Seventeen Kimbolton Terrace—'

Before Denny could say more, Joe cut him off. 'You're supposed to be working on Tandy Street.'

'Be fair, Joe. The work there's nearly done, we've gotta have something to keep the moolah coming in. And I told you, we're waiting of the gas man and leccy signing us off. Anyway, we bought this place at auction, the day before yesterday, and it needs a bit doing to it. New damp course, for starters, and we had to get the old plaster off the walls, rip out the laths and put new plasterboard up. Old boy next door came round whingeing that we'd brought plaster off his wall, too, so Tel went round to have a look, and got into an argument with the bloke. There were some cracks in his plaster, yeah, but they looked as if they were years old, so Tel told him to get stuffed.

End of story.' Denny gulped down more tea and appealed to Brenda. 'I'm starving. Any chance of a sausage butty to go with this, Brenda?'

'Sure, Denny. Three twenty-five to you.'

'Like I say, I'm not that hungry.'

Joe urged him on. 'Never mind looking for freebies. Get on with the tale.'

'About half past four this morning your niece, Gemma, knocked me up outta bed. They had Tel in the lockup, and she wanted the keys to search our van. Turns out he was on the razz last night—'

'When isn't he?' Joe interrupted.

'Yeah, well, he was too drunk to drive home, so he crashed at Kimbolton Terrace. According to Gemma, he swears he never heard anything, but about two in the morning, the street was flooded with cops, and some nosy neighbour pointed Tel out. That was it. Forensics have his dabs all over the old guy's house, and I'll bet they'll find his DNA, too, but that's because he was in there yesterday.'

'So what happened to the old boy?'

'Somebody bashed him over the head with a blunt instrument, which they haven't found yet, and that's why they wanted to search all our tools.'

'And you're sure it wasn't Tel?'

'Come off it, Joe. He doesn't mind the odd rumble, but he's no killer, and he wouldn't even bother with an old git like that.'

Joe drummed agitated fingers on the table top. With a week to Christmas, this was the last thing he needed. The café would be busy all day, they were already one short, and they could ill-afford his absence. He glanced up at Brenda, who had that stern, disapproving, yet resigned look in her eyes.

'You'd better see if you can sort it out,' she said.

'But what about the café?'

'We'll cope, won't we, Lee?'

'It's no problem, Uncle Joe. You get off and spring Tel.'

Joe nodded at Denny. 'All right. Leave it with me, I'll whip into town and have a word with Gemma, but I'm not promising anything. She rules the roost at Sanford police station these days, and she doesn't always listen to me.'

Denny finished his tea, got to his feet. 'You're sure there is no danger of that sausage butty?'

'Just get out, Denny, while you're in one piece. Bloody freeloaders. You're worse than the cops.'

Joe watched him leave and stood. 'I'd better get weaving if I'm gonna make it back in time to help with lunches. I'll be as quick as I can.'

He left his whites in the kitchen, put on his topcoat, and headed out through the rear door, climbed behind the wheel of his car, firing the engine, pulling away.

For anyone driving from The Lazy Luncheonette, getting to Sanford town centre was problematic. The café was situated in a parade on the southbound side of Doncaster Road, a dual carriageway, and from the café, there was no obvious means of turning right towards the town. Instead, Joe had to turn left at the nearest traffic lights, into the retail park, drive on for a hundred yards to a roundabout, where he doubled back, and returned to the same lights, from where he could turn right towards Sanford.

It was a pain at the best of times, but in the full-blooded flow of Christmas traffic, it was a nightmare, and Joe calculated that almost ten minutes passed before he was finally driving towards the town.

Things would not get any better. When the dual carriageway reduced to a single lane of two-way traffic, the traffic was heaving, and he lost a further five minutes as the cars, buses and lorries funnelled into a single line. Twenty minutes after leaving The Lazy Luncheonette, he arrived at the entry to the multi-storey car park at the Galleries Shopping Mall, where he joined yet another queue of slow-moving cars looking for parking spaces.

A full thirty minutes after he had made the decision, he stepped into Sanford Police Station, at the rear of the mall, asked for Detective Inspector Craddock, and eventually, his niece escorted him to her small office at the rear of the station.

It was a small, shabby room, one she had commandeered several years earlier as a detective sergeant. She had no window on the outside world, other than a small pane set high on one wall, which gave her a glimpse of brick walls beyond. She had, however, Christmas-ified the place with a small tree and several strings of tinsel here and there.

The season of goodwill had not extended to her personal demeanour. The moment they sat down, she guessed the reason for his call.

'Tel Bailey. Yeah?'

'Clever girl,' Joe congratulated her. 'I always knew you were smart.'

'Bandying compliments won't get you anywhere, Uncle Joe. What does he have to do with you anyway?'

'He and Denny are supposed to be doing up Tandy Street for me. He can't do that while he's walled up here something he didn't do, can he?'

Gemma waved a warning finger at him. 'We don't know whether or not he did it, so don't come the old "he's not guilty" routine. And, he's not here now. We let him go, provided he keeps us up to speed on his whereabouts. And to be honest, Uncle Joe, I don't care if he's rebuilding Tandy Street from scratch for you. An old man named Billy Trelfus died last night, Terry Bailey is in the frame, and that is my priority.'

Joe took the remonstration well. 'I assume you're waiting for forensic reports?'

'Yes.'

'Denny tells me that you've gone through their tools. Have you found the murder weapon?'

Jenner huffed out her breath in exasperation. 'You know, social media, text messages and email have nothing on the speed of the grapevine in this town. And like most social media, text and emails, it doesn't take long for the tale to get twisted. There is no murder weapon, Joe. Old man Trelfus died when he fell backwards and hit his head on the corner of a coffee table. It's more likely to be manslaughter than murder. Bailey says he wasn't anywhere near the old man last night, but we have witnesses who saw them arguing earlier in the day.'

'So Denny told me. And can you prove that Tel was there last night?'

'Not yet. But if he was, we'll get him.'

Joe considered the proposition. 'Do you have anyone else in the frame?'

'No. And before you get sticking your nose in, Tel's girlfriend can't vouch for him, either. The only thing she's been able to tell us is that he was completely blotto last night. Smashed out of his brains. She left him sleeping in the house and got a lift home.'

'In other words, she can't vouch…' Joe trailed off, his brow knitted into furrows of concentration. 'Girlfriend?'

'Ros Hepple. You know her. Archie, the auctioneer, his daughter.'

Joe nodded. 'Ah. I didn't know she and Tel had anything going down.'

'Not serious according to Ros. Just a few beers now and then.'

'And a bit of how's your father when Tel's sober enough.' Joe brought his rambling thoughts under control. 'All right. I'll go see what I can dig up.'

Gemma pointed the threatening finger again. 'Just be careful, Joe. Don't go poking your nose in too deeply. We get enough complaints from Kimbolton Terrace as it is. Builders, including Tel and Denny, are forever pestering the residents to sell up. They're worse than the texts and telephone cold-callers selling smart meters.'

A light lit in Joe's brain. 'Do you, now? I think that's really interesting. Don't you?'

'No I don't. It's a way of the world. Hassle, hassle, hassle, from everyone. Just watch your step.' Quite abruptly, Gemma changed the subject. 'How's Sheila?'

'Bad. We had Howard in earlier on telling us all about it. Apparently, her GP insists that it's all in her mind. Brenda and I are going to see her later.'

'And will you tell her what the doctor said?'

'Would you?' Joe laughed as he got to his feet. 'I'll catch you later, Gemma, and if I find anything out, you'll be the first to know... Oh. You don't happen to know where Tel was going when you let him out, do you?'

'He never said, but he can't go back to Kimbolton. Our people are there. So if Tandy Street is the only other job they have on their books...' Gemma trailed off, leaving the obvious suggestion hanging in the air.

With a mental reminder that he had not yet bought Gemma anything for Christmas, Joe left the police station, climbed back into his car, and joined the increasing traffic once again, but this time, instead of making for Doncaster Road, he headed west onto Leeds Road and at length turned into the maze of terraced streets running at right angles to the canal, and finally into Tandy Street, where the dark green, rusting, Bailey and Dixon van stood outside number twenty-three.

After the warmth of the car, the icy chill of the

morning snapped at his cheeks and hands. Buried in his winter coat, he shivered, and looked both ways along the street.

There was nothing in the way of traffic either moving along the street or passing along the bottom. There were cars parked outside several of the houses, and he noticed that curtains were closed at the occasional upper windows. Nightshift workers? If so, he guessed they would be none too happy to have him as a neighbour, starting up his noisy car at five o'clock every morning.

At the top end of the street a rough, stone wall blocked off access to the canal beyond, and Joe could imagine children generally making a nuisance of themselves at that end of the street, especially during the summer months, and the long break from school.

He decided he did not mind. His childhood had been spent in the apartment above the old Lazy Luncheonette, back in the days when it was known as Alf's Café. It had not been an unhappy time, but living on a main road precluded any possibility of playing in the street the way the children of Tandy Street would.

Putting aside his maudlin memories, he pushed open the door to number twenty-three and stepped in.

It was a hive of inactivity. The front room was bare, the walls stripped back to the plaster, ready for papering, the woodwork was sanded down in preparation for painting, but neither job could go ahead until Tel and Denny finished their work.

From the kitchen came the sound of muttered

voices, one of them grumpy, complaining (reminding Joe of himself more than anyone) the other whining, almost pleading.

He stepped in and found the two men in a corner by the back door. Denny was seated on a folding camping chair, Tel, hands clutched to his head, was perched on a stack of one-hundredweight plaster bags. In front of them was a primus stove, it's burner chuckling away, casting out a minimum amount of heat, and both men had already made tea or coffee from it.

'So this is what you get up to while my back's turned.'

It was as if they had only just registered his presence. Tel greeted him with a groan, Denny delivered a scathing look.

'Dinnertime, Joe. Or are you so busy serving meals you don't get chance to eat any?'

Joe ignored the jibe. 'What's the state of the parties?'

'We're in mufti. I told you earlier, we're waiting for a spark and the gas man to certify our work. Once that's done, we'll sign the place off, and you can call Alec Staines in to do the walls and paintwork.'

'Not much chance of me getting in this side of Christmas, then?'

Denny shrugged. 'Is your furniture ordered?'

'Yep. In storage of waiting for me to ring them and tell them to deliver.' He concentrated on Tel. 'Forget about the work for the minute, what about you?'

'What about me?'

They were not many men in Sanford prepared to argue with Tel Bailey. He was tall, fit and muscular, and notwithstanding his heavy drinking, he kept himself in the peak of condition with regular workouts at a local gym.

Joe, on the other hand, was one of the few who would challenge him. 'You were so tanked up last night that you don't even remember hassling Billy Trelfus?'

'Knock it off, Joe. I don't remember nothing. I didn't even know his name until your Gemma told me.'

Joe refused to back down. 'A man's dead. You're in the frame. Your only hope is to find the two active brain cells in your empty head, and start talking to me. I've just spoken to Gemma, and you're looking at a charge of manslaughter. Given your track record for scrapping, that's a good eight to ten years in the nick. Tell me what happened last night.'

'I already told you, I don't know.'

'I don't mean what happened at Kimbolton Terrace. Tell me what you did after you knocked off work for the day.'

He gave a shrug, and glanced around the dimly lit, barren room. 'I dunno. We wrapped up about six o'clock, Denny dropped me off at the gym on his way home. I spent an hour there, and then I met Ros in the Boat & Horses. We were on a promise after I helped out at the auction the other day.'

Denny fumed. 'Helped out? Poked his nose into the bidding. That's what he did. And all for a quick fumble with Ros.'

Joe pulled him up short. 'Don't let's get sidetracked. He's in enough trouble as it is.' He swung his attention to Tel. 'Go on.'

'I can't go on because that's all I remember. I was sinking a few, for sure. Whiskey chasers to help the beer go down, too. I think Ros walked me to Kimbolton. That's it. The next thing I knew, was the filth waking me up, chucking me in the paddy wagon, and carting me off down to Gale Street.' His brow cleared, and his eyes began to burn with certainty. 'I do know that I didn't go next door. Hassles like that wind me up, and I would have remembered. Not that your Gemma sees it like that. According to her, being drunk won't get me off.'

'She's right. Booze is no excuse in the eyes of the law.' Joe nudged him further along the sacks, and perched on the corner. 'Our Gemma tells me that the residents round here get a lot of hassle from guys like you, asking them to sell up so you can do the properties on to make a profit.'

It was Denny who answered. 'Not just us, Joe. Parsloe's one of the biggest culprits, and most of Sanford's builders are on the same game. If you can get a prop round here for, say, sixty-five grand, you can sell it on for at least a hundred a couple of months later. It's a paying game these days. And it's not just builders, you know. Archie Hepple sends canvassers out. He even does a bit himself, and they're only looking to auction the properties off. But, mark you, we've not done any door-knocking on Kimbolton for months. In fact, we haven't done any door-knocking since you called us in to do this job. And to my knowledge we never, ever knocked on Trelfus's door. He had a rep as a miserable old basket, and we can live without that kind of grief.'

'True enough,' Tel said. 'He was giving us some serious earache yesterday when we started knocking the plaster off the walls of number seventeen.'

'Yet Denny says the damage to his walls was nothing to do with you.'

'Nothing,' Tel confirmed. 'I went round and had a look at it, Joe, and some of those cracks are as old as you. Ask around if you don't believe me. I'll bet he's tried it with every builder in the town.'

'He still didn't deserve to die.' Joe stood up. 'All right, leave it with me. I'll make some enquiries, but hey, this is one you owe me. I'll expect you to get your finger out and get this place finished before the courts send Tel down for the next ten years.'

Tel groaned. 'Oh, God, no.'

'You want some advice, lad? I know for a fact that you won't listen, but the best thing you can do is get off the beer. Marry Archie's daughter and settle down, because one of these days, you'll find yourself in a worse position than this, and there won't be a friendly Joe Murray around to save you.'

Chapter Four

Joe arrived back at The Lazy Luncheonette a little after half past twelve, as the lunchtime rush was picking up, and for the next hour he was too busy to give his crew anything but the barest details of Tel Bailey's predicament.

'I promise to look further into it,' he said to Brenda, as he placed a customer's order for a chicken and salad sandwich and poured out a cup of tea to go with it. 'As long as you guys can cope.'

'Bad without Sheila.'

'We could always give that Russian lass, that Nadia, a shout, Uncle Joe,' Lee called from the kitchen.

Nadia had joined them briefly after the affair at Squires Lodge, but she found the pressure of working at full stretch too much, and she had moved on to secure a permanent, if part-time cleaning job.

'Forget it,' Brenda said. 'A nice enough girl, but she could never master the difference between steak and kidney pudding and sticky toffee pudding. I don't know how many customers complained that their dessert was covered in gravy. We'll manage, Joe. Provided you're here to help with breakfast, we can cope with the rest of the day.'

By two o'clock, the rush was over, and the afternoon calm began to set in. At half past two, just as he and Brenda were preparing to leave to visit Sheila, Joe's mobile rang. He checked the menu window, and read Eliot Banks, the senior claims investigator at North Shires Insurance, a company which Denise Latham had introduced him to before her untimely death.

'What the hell does he want?' Joe made the connection and put the phone to his ear. 'Eliot. What can I do you for?'

'I've a job for you, Joe, if you're interested.'

'Right now, I'm up to my neck in staff chucking a sickie, my builder accused of murder, and the Christmas rush. Is it important?'

'Top priority. It'll pay you a handsome five grand and a percentage of any monies we recoup if you can pull it off. Can you get to Leeds to see me?'

Joe clucked impatiently. 'Tell you what, it'll either be tomorrow or very late this afternoon, say half past five, six o'clock.'

'Today. I'll wait for you. Soon as you can, please, Joe.'

'More hassle?' Brenda asked as he killed the connection.

'More work. I should've stayed in the Canary Islands with Alison. I could have been enjoying winter sunshine right now.'

Brenda cackled. 'You mean you could have been enjoying Alison.'

'Yuk.' Joe delivered his misleading, tongue in cheek opinion as he put on his coat and hinted that Brenda should get ready.

After fleeing Palmanova he had made his way

by a roundabout route to Tenerife, where he met up with his ex-wife, and Alison had been good to him. She had even pressured him into staying there permanently, and at those times when he thought about it, he often wondered how things would have panned out had he taken her up on the offer.

Outside the café, he and Brenda climbed into their separate cars, for the two-mile drive to Sheila's bungalow.

Larch Avenue was on the north-western side of Sanford, a slightly more affluent area than the terraced streets Joe was proposing to move into. Sheila had lived there for most of her married life, and she maintained her bungalow even after her first husband's death.

But for signs that two cars were usually parked in the drive, little had changed in the external appearance of the house. The front lawn, declining into its winter sadness, was closely cropped, lined with herbaceous borders, all of them, once again, without flowers, the hedgerow dividing her property with that of her neighbour, was in need of trimming, but that aside, everything was as it had always been.

Matters were no different at the rear, where the lawn stretched all the way from the patio to the dishevelled hedgerows, and where a small apple tree showed sad, barren branches. The rear entrance to the garden comprised a tall, stout wooden gate, badly in need of a coat of creosote.

If nothing was different outside, the interior had seen marked changes. As Howard had told them, all pictures of Peter had been removed, except for one which adorned the wall of the narrow hall when they first entered, and even then, Sheila and her late husband were visible only as members of the party attending Brenda's wedding to her late husband, Colin. The major change, however, was in the living room, where a large, silver-framed photograph of Sheila and Martin, taken outside the church on their wedding day, dominated the shelf above the fireplace.

A five-foot Christmas tree stood in one corner, its lights flashing amiably, and various other decorations were scattered about the wall. Joe had always considered it unusual since both her sons lived in America, and although she would love to be with them, he knew that Sheila preferred Christmas at home.

On the one occasion he had asked, she explained, 'I speak to them regularly over video links, but especially on Christmas morning, and my grandchildren like to see the house properly decorated.'

Now, she appeared pale, drawn, and it seemed to both Brenda and Joe that she had lost weight; the difficult feat to achieve considering her already slender lines. Clad only in a nightdress with a fluffy gown wrapped around her, she directed Joe to the kitchen, asking him to make her a weak tea without milk, and standard brews for himself and Brenda, and led her best friend into the living room, where she cowered in an armchair by the glowing gas fire.

When Joe joined them, Brenda was on the corner of the three-seat settee closest to Sheila, and when he had distributed the cups of tea, he took the seat on the other end of the couch.

Brenda wasted little time on small talk, and asked how Sheila had come to this situation.

'The Cape Verde Islands. I had this local dish. *Arroz de Marisco.*' Sheila pronounced it in an almost perfect Spanish/Portuguese accent. 'It's a sort of Portuguese paella, and I'm not saying there was anything wrong with it, but you know me. I prefer traditional British cooking.'

'Joe's home-made steak and kidney pudding,' Brenda said.

Sheila raised a weak smile. 'I wouldn't go that far.' She received a scowl from the object of her teasing. 'But ever since I had this meal, I've not been right.' She gazed sadly through the windows. 'It must be awful for Martin. Here we are, married just three months, and he's saddled with a wife who falls sick at the drop of a hat.'

Joe's smartphone bleated for attention, and he cut the call off, but not without checking the menu window and registering a call from Tel Bailey. He apologised to Sheila. 'Not urgent. I can get back to him.'

Ignoring the interruption, Brenda was keen to reassure her friend. 'Martin sounded very concerned when we spoke to him this morning.'

'He is,' Sheila said. 'I feel so sorry for him, Brenda, but he's a paragon of patience.' For the second time she smiled at Joe. 'I'm sure you could learn a few lessons from him.'

'Nice try, Sheila, but I'm too concerned about you to let you wind me up. I don't want you worrying about your wages or your profit share. They'll be there, as always.'

'To be honest, money is the least of my worries. But you're very kind.'

Joe leapt upon the opportunity to tease her for a change. 'I know I am, but don't go telling everyone.'

Sheila took a sip of tea as her stomach gurgled audibly. 'I'm sorry. I can't help it.'

'Then stop apologising for it,' Brenda suggested.

Sheila's sadness showed through again despite her obvious attempts to suppress it. 'I was going to invite you both for Christmas lunch. Well, you both live alone, and although I know we usually make our own arrangements—'

'Yes,' Brenda interrupted. 'You usually come to my place, or vice versa.'

'And I usually end up with Lee, Cheryl and young Danny,' Joe said.

'I was saying,' Sheila went on, irritably, 'I was going to invite you for lunch on Christmas Day, but I'm not sure I'll be well enough.'

'Let's change the plans, then. If you're up to it, bring Martin along to my place for a good, old fashioned knees-up,' Brenda insisted, 'and I'll invite Joe along. Short of a donkey, we need something to pin the tail on.'

Joe ignored the badinage. He desperately wanted to bring up Howard's opinions. Brenda had warned him not to mention it, and he agreed. In his balance sheet, when tallying up the pluses and minuses, diplomacy was firmly in the column headed "Liabilities". Resisting the urge to open his mouth (and put his foot in it) he nevertheless told her of Howard's visit to The Lazy Luncheonette.

'He was always more considerate than his mother,' Sheila responded. 'If Rita were still with us and I told her about my troubles, it would eventually turn into a debate on her health problems.'

'Have I told you about my bad back?' Joe said, and grinned at her. 'Do you think you'll be well enough for Churchill's tomorrow night?'

It was an aspect none of them had thought about. It had only just occurred to Joe. Thursday was the traditional 3rd Age Club's Christmas dinner and dance held at Sanford's finest restaurant/nightspot.

Sheila's face fell. 'I don't want to commit myself, Joe.'

'Well, you have your tickets. If you don't think you can make it, let me know, and I'll see if I can sell them to someone else.'

'Howard and Gemma,' Brenda suggested brightly.

'Hardly third-agers,' Joe protested, 'and they're not members of the club.'

'Neither is Martin, but it didn't stop you selling me a ticket for him,' Sheila reminded him.

Joe gave up the unequal battle. Whenever he got into a debate with the two women, he invariably lost the argument. 'All right. Whatever. Listen, Sheila, I don't want you coming back to work until you're absolutely well, and if that means sometime in the New Year, then so be it.

We'll cope.'

'I miss you two more than anything else. I enjoy the banter in the café. I even enjoy your snaps and snarls, Joe. I'm really sorry, and I want to get back as soon as I can.'

Joe patted her hand sympathetically. 'Take it easy. Get yourself right. No hurry.'

It was almost half past four and night had already fallen by the time he and Brenda came out to their respective cars, and at Joe's suggestion, they pulled out of the street, around the corner, away from Sheila's prying eyes before they stopped, and he climbed into the passenger seat of Brenda's Peugeot.

She ran the engine to keep warm, and asked, 'What do you think?'

'I think Howard and her doctor were talking a load of hot air. Did you see how pale and pasty she looked? That's not in her mind, Brenda. There's something seriously wrong with that woman.'

'But if that's the case, Joe, they would have traced it by now.'

Joe drummed irritable fingers on his knee caps. 'I don't know. They're not perfect you know, these medics. They can miss things.' He quickly changed the subject. 'Can we manage, do you think? Or should we get some help in? At the café, I mean.'

'I think we'll definitely need to bring in some of Cheryl's friends. What with you flying off to investigate this and that murder, it'll probably be too much for us, but I'll keep an eye on things.'

'Right.' Joe prepared to leave the car and

return to his own. 'I'd better shoot off to Leeds, and I'll see you first thing in the morning.'

* * *

Even with a hands-free option, Joe was reluctant to use his phone while driving, but as he ran down the M1 into central Leeds, smack in the middle of the rush hour, a level of traffic compounded by the extra pressure of Christmas shoppers, he made an exception and returned Tel's call, only to discover that the elite builder was ringing to apologise.

'Yeah, Joe, it was Denny who said I should ring you, cos I was a bit short with you earlier.'

Joe grunted. 'If you want snappy, you should try me behind the counter of The Lazy Luncheonette first thing on the morning. Just forget it, Tel, and concentrate your mind and recalling every tiny thing you can about last night. I'm on my way to Leeds right now, but tomorrow, I'll get hold of Ros Hepple and see what she can tell me.'

North Shires had their offices on Park Row, the main banking and insurance area of the city, but it was a one-way street, and only the upper half was accessible to traffic other than buses. It meant fighting his way right round the city centre, to approach from The Headrow, across the front of the magnificent town hall. At this hour, the streets were clogged with a constant stream of headlights, augmenting the spread of Christmas illuminations hung both above the streets and glowing from shop windows.

Joe had met ex-Detective Sergeant Denise Latham when she was investigating the fire which burned down the old Lazy Luncheonette, and she had helped prove Joe innocent. More than that, she was instrumental in exposing the real arsonists/murderers. From there, a firm friendship had developed, turning almost inevitably into a relationship, and Joe was happy to be with her. He even helped with her investigations, most of which were on behalf of North Shires. When she was killed in a car accident (which later proved to be deliberate and a case of murder) North Shires offered Joe the opportunity to take on her work. He did not exactly decline, but he remained choosy about the cases he was willing to accept.

Since then, he had developed a good working relationship with the company's senior investigator, Eliot Banks. Banks freely admitted that he preferred to use men and women who had seen service with the police, but like many people, he readily acknowledged Joe's deductive skills and intuitive leaps to the correct conclusion. He also paid excellent rates which helped offset Joe's reduction in income when he had to pay Lee, Sheila and Brenda their share of The Lazy Luncheonette's quarterly performance.

Getting to North Shires, especially in the rush-hour was no easy task. Long before he made the final right turn into Park Row, his frustration was manifesting in muttered curses and agitated gestures to other road users. The cost of a pay-and-display car park did little to appease his annoyance, and by the time he confronted a security guard inside the North Shires' building, he was at boiling point.

'He never told me he was expecting you.'

'He keeps you abreast of all his appointments, does he?'

The security man was suitably offended. 'I'm here to keep toe rags like you out of the building.'

'Even when one of the big bosses is expecting me? Just get on the phone to him, you clown, and tell him Joe Murray's here.'

'If you're ragging me…'

With this unspoken threat hanging in the air, the security officer spoke to Banks, and Joe was finally allowed to go on his way.

For all that the company was housed in an impressive ten-storey office block, in the heart of the city's financial district, its front windows overlooking Part Row, and the wide open City Square, complete with Christmas decorations, Banks's fourth-floor office was at the rear of the building, and looked out onto a dingy yard littered with dustbins, and a small smoke shelter.

Eliot Banks was somewhere around forty years of age. A tall, square-shouldered man with a rough edge to his voice. The fingers of his large hands were decked with various gold rings, and behind the open collar of his white shirt and the loosely hanging, red, company tie, a thick, gold chain dangled around his neck. It was all designed to intimidate; to give the impression of a late-model, tough street cop, even though most people were aware that Banks had never been in the police service. Joe did not know him well, but based on Denise's basic biography of him, he knew that Banks had some military service behind him, and he was excellent at his job, uncompromising, and not afraid of pushing the edge of the envelope in order to prevent fraud.

He waved Joe into an empty seat, and held up a bottle of Johnny Walker.

Joe declined. 'I'll catch up with the booze in the Miner's Arms tonight. You said you had something for me.'

'I do,' Banks said, pouring a generous measure of whiskey into a beaker.

To Joe, the gesture had more to do with the man's posing as a wannabe cop, and as if to reinforce it, Banks took a healthy swallow, dropped the beaker on the desk and leaned back in his chair.

'The case is a good few years old, Joe, and North Shires did settle at the time, even though there were a lot of questions unanswered. Fifty thousand quid. And that happened – we think – not once but twice. Course, I wasn't with the company at that time, and I might have dug a little bit deeper into it than the company or even the cops.'

'Don't think I'm being picky, Eliot, but you're not saying what this is about.'

'Yeah. Right. Murder, Joe. That's what it's about. The police said no… at least in one case they did. Initially they couldn't prove anything in the second, but we eventually showed them the error of their ways. Trouble is, the cops can't find the perpetrator, and I'm keen to prevent it happening a third time.'

Joe applied his mind, and waded through the disparate elements of the tale. 'Right, so you know who he is, and where he is, and who he's gonna kill next?'

'No, yes, yes. I don't know for sure that he's the right man, but I do know where he is, and I know who his next victim is likely to be, and if I'm not mistaken, she's a friend of yours.'

Joe laughed nervously. 'That doesn't leave you with many options. There aren't many people I can call friends.'

'How about Sheila Riley?'

Joe gaped. 'Sheila?'

Banks nodded grimly. 'If I'm right, Joe, she doesn't have long to live.'

Chapter Five

Joe's head whirled. He reached across the desk, took the bottle and swallowed a slug from the neck. 'Are you off your trolley? Sheila? She's just got married.'

Banks remained comfortably superior. 'I know. And that's what put me onto her.'

He sat upright in his seat, and opened the file on his desk. From his poor vantage point, Joe could see that one of the documents was a photocopy of a page from the Sanford Gazette, and it detailed Sheila's marriage back in September, carrying a page-wide photograph of her, her new husband, and one or two of those in attendance, including Joe, Brenda, and Sheila's two sons.

'Contrary to popular opinion, we don't just sit on our backsides waiting for things to happen here,' Banks went on. 'We do our homework. I meanersay, why am I still here at getting on for six o'clock, on a December evening, when I could be home putting my feet up? Homework is why. Denise used to talk a lot about you and your friends, Brenda and Sheila, and I happened to be skimming through the Sanford Gazette when I noticed her wedding photograph.'

Joe frowned. 'What puzzles me more than anything is you taking the Sanford Gazette here in Leeds. I live in Sanford, and I don't always bother with it.'

Banks went on to list other provincial

newspapers which he took on a regular basis, from cities like Wakefield and York, and towns like Huddersfield, Dewsbury, Harrogate, and as far afield as Scarborough and Hull to the East, Rochdale and Skipton to the West.

'I spend some of my time reading these things, Joe, because I never know what I might come across, and my job is all about preventing fraud, and if I can't prevent it, then proving it and bringing it to the courts.' Banks tapped the photocopy of the Sanford Gazette. 'When I looked at this photograph, I recognised Martin Naylor right away, only according to our records his name is Mervyn Nellis, and thirteen years ago, his first wife disappeared without trace.'

Joe's quelled his immediate anxiety for Sheila's safety. 'The murder you couldn't prove?'

'The very same. It's difficult to prove murder when you don't have a body, and Francine Nellis, nee Varanne didn't leave us a body. She was French by birth, and when the police questioned Nellis, he insisted that she just took off one day, and he never saw or heard from her again. He assumed that she'd gone back to France, but immigration had no trace of passport ever being used, and the French police were about as much use as ours. They couldn't find her, her family never heard anything from her, and that was it. Seven years down the line, she was declared legally dead, and North Shires had no option but to pay up. Fifty grand. At the time, Nellis lived in Darlington, but the minute he got his grubby little paws on the cash, he disappeared, too, and we never heard anything of him again. Then five years ago, a man named Marlon Newman took out a fifty thousand pounds policy on his partner, a lady named Deirdre Ullsworth. They were quite happily living together in a nice little house on the outskirts of Ripon. Two years down the line, Deirdre had a heart attack. She was a teacher, and we all know the kind of pressure they're under. She was in her mid-fifties at the time, so it wasn't entirely unexpected. A couple of weeks after she'd been discharged from hospital, she had a second heart attack and died. No post-mortem necessary. Marlon Newman took time out of his grief to claim the insurance, and North Shires paid up. This was just before I was appointed head of fraud, and I reviewed the case along with others, including Francine Nellis. Marlon Newman looks remarkably like Mervyn Nellis, and both of them bear a striking resemblance to Martin Naylor.'

To support his assertion, Banks placed two photographs and the photocopy on the desk, and turned all three to face Joe who could see the likeness immediately. They were the same height, had the same slender, but athletic build, but Mervyn Nellis sported shoulder length hair, while Marlon Newman was possessed of a full set, beard and moustache, and Martin Naylor's hair was neatly trimmed, and he was clean shaven.

Joe recalled Sheila's words on the afternoon she had asked him to escort her down the aisle. *Martin isn't from Sanford. He's not even a Yorkshireman.* Nellis, Newman, call him what you will, originated from Darlington, and although it was borderline, Darlington was not a part of Yorkshire.

His fear for Sheila's life returned, and he urged Banks, 'You have to tell the police.'

The other man shrugged his broad shoulders. 'Based on what, Joe? Three men who look alike. Neither Nellis nor Newman are on any DNA database. Nellis was, true, but when his wife's disappearance was ruled as nothing more sinister than that, he insisted on the record being destroyed, which it was. We did get onto the police in Ripon after Deirdre died and I'd rumbled the similarities. They exhumed the body, and did a post-mortem on what was left of her. Speculative, but it shouted atropine poisoning. Course, by this time, Marlon Newman had sold Deirdre's house for the better part of two hundred grand, taken another fifty k off North Shires, and disappeared without trace. As far as the cops are concerned, it is murder, but it's a cold case because they can't find Newman. And you and I both know why they can't find him, don't we?'

'Because he never existed in the first place.'

'Spot on,' Banks agreed.

'Difficult, though, getting work with a false ID. Especially in a school where they chase up references.'

'Difficult, yes, impossible, no,' Banks said. 'Remember, Joe, he copped a tidy sum seven years after Francine disappeared.'

'And did the Ripon police drag the Darlington squad in on it?'

Banks shook his head. 'As far as I'm aware,

they ran a query with them, but if they made any enquiries, we were never told about them, which, as far as I'm concerned, means they just asked a few questions about it. This old chicken had been missing for the better part of ten years at that stage, they weren't likely to have any more joy than the original investigators.' Banks relaxed again, and collecting photographs and photocopy, closed the file. 'If I'm right, Joe, your friend, Mrs Riley, Naylor, whatever she wants to call herself, is in serious danger. If I'm wrong, well, you'll just make me look a complete berk.'

Joe grinned without humour. 'Trust me, I don't stop to worry about things like that. One thing puzzles me, Eliot. Since when is a large company like North Shires concerned for the safety of people who are not their customers?'

Banks laughed. 'Mrs Riley is a customer. Sorry, did I not mention it? She took out a large policy with us after her husband died. Two hundred and fifty thousand pounds. If I'm right, Joe, not only will you lose a friend, but North Shires will lose a bloody fortune.'

Joe needed no more incentive, but the hard-headed Yorkshireman would not let him leave it there. 'And you're offering me five grand?'

'You need a sweetener? I told you you'd be on a percentage. For every penny we can recover from Nellis/Newman/Naylor, I'll throw in a one percent bonus.'

Joe glanced down at the file. 'Do I get a copy of the full report?'

Banks reached into a drawer of his desk, came

out with a folder similar to the one spread on his desk. He handed it over. 'Absolutely confidential, Joe. No one must see it but you.' He paused a moment, his brow creasing. 'Although come to think, I'm told that you have contacts in the police.'

Joe took the folder and nodded as he got to his feet. 'My niece, Detective Inspector Craddock, Sanford CID, and her boyfriend, DI Howard Riley of Leeds CID. Sheila's nephew.'

Banks blanched. 'For God's sake don't let him see that lot, not until you've got some evidence. If he goes tramping in with his size thirteens, and we've got it wrong, he could wreck his aunt's marriage for nothing.'

* * *

Joe got back to his car just after six o'clock. The evening traffic showed no inclination to thin out. If anything, it appeared busier, and he guessed that many people would have finished work, and set about Christmas shopping.

As he climbed behind the wheel, started the engine, switching the heaters to full to combat the biting cold of the winter's night, he was oblivious to the bright lights and Yuletide glitz around him. The last thing on his mind was Christmas.

He had met Martin Naylor on many occasions after Sheila's summer announcement of her forthcoming marriage, and he had never found the man anything but pleasant company. But that meant nothing. How many murderers had he encountered who were superficially pleasant and outgoing? Many of them were women, some had even succeeded in seducing him. But behind the facade was always a calculating, cold-blooded killer. Masks, like those of the Santas stood outside many of Leeds's department stores, were too easy to put in place, too simple to maintain in public, too easy to let slip when the time was right.

Pangs of hunger reminded him that he had eaten nothing since a rushed meal in The Lazy Luncheonette. He joined the queues of traffic again, fought his way into a multi-storey car park just off Briggate, arguably Leeds's busiest shopping thoroughfare, and once parked up, joined the thousands thronging the streets.

He ambled into Trinity Shopping Mall, and partly in a daze, passed familiar High Street names, shops which will be found in virtually any town or city in the country. Eventually, he settled into a corner of a fast-food joint, and chewed through a tasteless burger and fries, washing it down with tea that tasted more like warm water, and for once his thoughts were not on how much better he could produce such fare. They were centred entirely on Sheila.

Across the way, children gambolled in the queue to see Santa. Young people, whose lives had barely just begun, and their unbridled excitement carried him back across the years to the days when he had been a similar age, had felt the same excitement, had joined the queues along with other, firm friends, amongst whom were Sheila and Brenda.

He remembered the thrill of getting nearer and nearer, and telling Santa what he wanted for Christmas, promising to be the goodest of the good little boys, and the joy of collecting a real, genuine gift from Father Christmas. He took his great nephew, Danny, to see Santa in Sanford's Galleries Shopping Mall every year, and found the boy's excitement to be contagious; he loved it as much as Danny, as much as he, Sheila and Brenda had at that age.

He was fond of saying that it takes a lifetime to make a true friend, and despite their many disagreements (most of them minor) over the years those two women were true friends. There were others, Alec and Julia Staines, George Robson, Owen Frickley, even, heaven help him, Les Tanner and his ladylove, Sylvia Goodson; men and women who would stand at his side in Sheila's defence.

But what if Banks had it wrong? A true friend she might be, but Sheila was a strict and frequently unforgiving woman. She would never tolerate such allegations without some foundation. If Joe fired from the hip, half a century of friendship would be in tatters.

He climbed back into his car at half past seven, his mind still tumbling with indecision, and as he started the engine, began the slow crawl out of the car park, onto the busy streets, he hooked his phone into the car speakers, called Brenda, and asked her to meet him in the Miner's Arms an eight o'clock.

He met]with fierce resistance. 'I'd planned on

having a night in. We've Churchill's tomorrow night, remember.'

'Yeah. With the weekly disco cancelled, so had I, but something's come up, and I need to speak to you urgently, Brenda, because I don't know how to handle it.'

The announcement ignited her worries. 'What? What is it?'

'I don't wanna talk over the phone, and anyway, I'm driving, but it's urgent. Trust me. Just meet me in the Miner's at eight and I'll bring you up to speed.'

* * *

About half a mile from The Lazy Luncheonette, the Miner's Arms had stood on Doncaster Road since the days when the pit was one of the major employers in Sanford. When it was up and running, the actual mine was on the other side of town, and many people had pointed the anomaly out.

Licensee, Mick Chadwick, was unrepentant. Plenty of the men employed at the pit had lived on this side of Sanford, and no one ever complained about the naming of the Foundry Inn. For those daring enough to point out that the Foundry Inn was within a few hundred yards of where the old foundry had stood, Mick's response was short, snappy, and often unsuitable for mixed company.

The pub's position, at the point on Doncaster Road where the industrial estate tapered off, and the residential areas of South Sanford began, was ideal, and from Mick's point of view, profitable. He had his ups and downs, but over the year, he made a more than adequate gains, none more so than Wednesday evenings when Sanford 3rd Age Club held their weekly disco in the top room. Not only did he charge the club for use of the room, but sales of drinks and snacks shot up well above the average.

There were those times of the year, however, when the third agers cancelled the disco, and when Mick looked at his sales figures, it was enough to bring on one of his petulant moods, and both his wife, Beth and the other bar staff knew to give him a wide berth. One such occasion was the week of the annual Sanford 3rd Age Club Christmas Dinner & Dance, always held at Churchill's. The club membership, most of whom were either pensioners or approaching pension age, would not tolerate two evenings of comparative excess, and as a result, the weekly disco was cancelled.

When Joe arrived a couple of minutes before eight, Mick was already in full moan mode.

'The pennies you spend won't make up for the money I'm losing tonight.'

'You know what I love about you, Mick? You're a thoroughbred Yorkshireman. Nothing matters but the weight of your wallet.'

Placing a half of lager and a Campari and soda in front of Joe, Mick retorted, 'I wish I was making a fraction the amount you make out of that café.'

'Yes, but with me to get serious insults, not your half-hearted snaps.'

Nodding a passing "hello"' to one or two people, Joe retired to an empty table in the far corner of the lounge bar, and checked the near empty room. Mick was right. There were less than a dozen people in the lounge, and only a few more in the public bar where a live football match was on TV. Normally, this bar would be packed with club members, waiting for the top room to open, and the landlord would be lucky to cover the cost of electricity and heating with the evening's takings.

Wrapped in a heavy, quilted coat, but nevertheless shivering, Brenda walked into the room five minutes later, glanced around, and joined him. 'This had better be worth it, Joe Murray,' she said, removing her coat and sitting alongside him. 'You've dragged me away from a night of serious channel hopping on the telly.'

'Yes, well, I'd planned to cut my toenails, but after speaking to Eliot Banks, I have more important things on my mind.'

Brenda sipped her Campari. 'So fill me in.'

Given Brenda's free lifestyle, Joe would have chuckled at the inevitable innuendo in her words, but Banks's information had been preying on his mind ever since he left the offices of North Shires. Over the next quarter of an hour, he told Brenda everything, and showed her the documents Banks had given him. As the tale unfolded, she became first, more serious, and then with the revelation of the murdered woman and the missing first wife, it turned to look of pure dread. Finally, when Joe finished the tale, the only emotion he could read in her face was thrilling anger. 'If he's poisoning Sheila, I'll rip his wedding tackle off and nail it to his head.'

'Yeah, yeah, yeah. I feel the same way, but we have to think seriously about this, Brenda. We have absolutely no proof that Martin Naylor is Mervyn Nellis or Marlon Newman.'

Brenda slapped a hand down on the photographs causing one or two people to look in their direction. 'It's him, Joe. You only have to look at the pictures to see it.'

'They look alike, granted, it's difficult to be certain, and you know what I'm concerned about, don't you? Sheila's reaction if we get it wrong.'

The announcement drew Brenda up short. It was obvious that she had not considered that aspect. 'Oh dear. Yes. She'll tear you and me into little pieces, and then feed us through a shredder, and then sweep us into the gutter.' She took another swallow of Campari. 'We've been friends for so long. All of us.' She turned appealing eyes on him. 'What are we going to do, Joe? If he is the same man, we can't leave her at his mercy.'

Joe took in more lager. 'It's difficult. We'll be walking on eggshells. And what makes it more complicated is that the medics haven't actually found anything wrong with Sheila. If he was poisoning her, it would have shown up in the tests, but according to what Howard told us, and Sheila herself said, there's nothing to account for the problem.'

'Untraceable poison?' Brenda asked more in hope than certainty.

'No such thing according to my knowledge. Any poison would show up provided the medics do their job properly, and I can't see them shirking the work, can you?'

Silence fell between them, punctuated only by the rattle of bottles and glasses behind the bar, the muted hum of conversation from a few patrons in the lounge, and the chatter of football fans from the public.

Brenda broke it. 'Could Howard help?'

Joe's drummed his fingers on his lips. 'Possible, I suppose. At least as a bona fide police officer, he could look into it and possibly pull Martin in for questioning, but I don't think he'd get very far. Martin would only deny it, and the cops have no DNA on file from either Nellis or Newman.'

Brenda made up her mind. 'In that case, it's up to you and me. What say we collar Martin and give him the third degree?' She could see the doubt in his features. 'Come on, Joe. Sheila is our oldest friend, and she very dear to both of us. We can't leave her in danger, and let's be honest about this, when it comes to facing people down, you have no equal. All right, so when it comes to fighting, if you tried to take toffees from a newborn baby, you'd lose, but you're not afraid of hassling anyone, with me alongside you, Martin wouldn't dare get physical.'

'What would a newborn baby be doing with toffees?' Joe still had his doubts. 'We'll have to bring in extra staff at The Lazy Luncheonette.'

'Lee and Cheryl can arrange that. Even if

she's ill, Cheryl can call on her friends, and Lee might be a bit of a dipstick, but he knows how to run the place.'

He made up his mind. 'All right. We'll get breakfast out the way tomorrow, then leave it to Lee while we shoot over to Sanford Park Comprehensive, and tackle Martin. Agreed?'

'Agreed.'

Chapter Six

Harold Ogilvy was a couple of years older than Joe and Brenda, and had been headmaster (or Principal as he preferred to call himself) of Sanford Park Comprehensive for the last decade. Under his guidance, the school plodded its way through the usual crises involved in the education of teenagers, but he was always pleased to welcome former pupils.

Situated in a green belt in the eastern half of Sanford, it was a vast expanse of playing fields surrounding the glass and concrete main buildings. In those far-off days when Joe and Brenda had attended the school, it was known as Sanford Secondary Modern, but even then, the brighter pupils, amongst whom were Sheila and Brenda, sat their GCE, O and A-levels, and some went on to university. Others, like Brenda, settled for a career in banking, while Sheila opted for secretarial college and eventually joined the school's administrative staff, where she remained for most of her working life, eventually rising to the vaunted position of school secretary.

Joe never had the option. True, he sat his O-level exams, and came away with a couple of passes in English and maths, but on leaving school at the age of sixteen he became a full-time employee of The Lazy Luncheonette, or Alf's Café as it was known then. Not that his education ended at that point. His father insisted that he went on to catering college on a part-time basis, where he studied for three years.

At any time in his life, he could have cut away from the family business and taken work as a chef in more upmarket eateries, but allied to his cooking skills was a sharp, financial acuity which showed him the way forward. When his older brother, Arthur, moved to Australia, Joe realised that the family business would come to him when his father retired or passed away. Now through his mid-fifties, he had never seen any reason to regret his decision.

Ogilvy commented on it when they joined him in his comfortable office overlooking the playing fields. 'Given the plethora of cookery programmes on TV, you could have had your own show by now.'

'Yes, but I'd have had to learn to speak proper English, like what the Queen does, Harold, and I'm a common Sanforder at heart.'

As always, it had been a busy morning, with the Sanford Brewery drivers clogging up the café from a little after seven o'clock until half past eight, and it was almost an hour after that before Joe and Brenda could leave the running of the place to Lee and his wife Cheryl, who appeared to be fully recovered from whatever ailed her the previous day. Cheryl, a sociable, likeable woman, much more astute and focused than her lumbering husband, had brought in two of her friends to help out, allowing Joe and Brenda the opportunity to get on their way to the school.

When they arrived, they were compelled to

wait until Ogilvy was through with the morning's disciplinary matters, dealing with recalcitrant students and (according to him) staff.

'It's the time of year,' he had explained with a heavy sigh and by way of apology. 'We break up for Christmas tomorrow, and to be honest, no one is getting through a great deal of work, and that includes the staff. I imagine you're rushed off your feet.'

'Burning out the soles of his trainers,' Brenda chuckled.

Ogilvy smiled by return. 'So what can I do… Oh. Forgive me. How's is Mrs Naylor? Martin told me she was very ill, and has been ever since they came back from Cape Verde.'

It took Brenda a moment to register Sheila's identity from her new, married surname. She still thought of her as Sheila Riley. 'Still queasy, and as it happens, that's why we're here. I know it may be inconvenient, Harold, but would it be possible to speak to Martin?'

Ogilvy frowned. 'Is it urgent?'

'Very,' Joe assured him.

It seemed to Joe that the headmaster deliberately set his face in a mask of disapproval and concern while he checked the master timetable on his computer.

'He's currently with year ten, leading them on a drama production designed to be put on by Easter. They're in rehearsal in the assembly hall, and I don't suppose he'll mind you interrupting.' Ogilvy checked his watch. 'There's only another ten or fifteen minutes to morning break.' He smiled obsequiously at them. 'You know the way?'

'Unless you've redesigned the place,' Joe said, and he and Brenda left the headmaster's office.

They ambled along the first floor corridor, taking in the noticeboards carrying photographs of Head Girl and Head Boy, and the duly appointed prefects, intermingled with photographs of staff members, heads of departments, and at the top of the virtual family tree, Ogilvy himself, his photograph labelled with his name and a line of qualifications, most of which meant little to Joe.

'You never got your face on the noticeboard, Joe?'

He grunted. 'Yes I did. But only as a horrible example to everyone else.'

They cast the occasional glance through the upper, glass halves of classroom doors, where pupils appeared as model schoolchildren, their full attention on their class teachers. Joe Rather doubted it and said so.

'Five'll get you ten, the little swines are passing notes, and plotting anarchy.'

'Texts, these days.' Brenda laughed. 'And are you showing off your photographic memory again? In our year, the notes were all from you, George Robson and Owen Frickley… oh, and Alec Staines. Proper gang of thugs you lot were.'

The assembly hall/gymnasium was on the ground floor, and as Ogilvy promised, Martin Naylor was leading a drama group, and called a brief halt to the performance to welcome them.

The gym equipment had been moved to one side of the hall, and a group of about fifteen pupils at around in a semicircle while Martin stood between them and the stage, where two teenage boys were listening to him. Joe recognised one of the youngsters as Amir Patel, a young man whose father had owned the minimarket next door to the original Lazy Luncheonette before it burned down. Amir cast Joe a toothy grin, and Joe waved back.

And it was to Amir that Martin was speaking. 'It's not kilt, Amir, but killed. "I've killed him," not "I've kilt him". You make it sound as if you dressed your victim up as a Scotsman.'

The comment send a ripple of laughter round the fifteen or so students in the group, and Martin turned his attention to the two visitors.

'Joe, Brenda, nice to see you both.' He cast a glance at his watch. 'We're almost due for morning break.'

Brenda smiled bleakly. 'We can hang on a few minutes, Martin.'

They took seats on one of a long benches used for assembly, now stacked up at the rear of the room, while the teacher and students went on rehearsing whatever the play was.

'I don't recognise it,' Joe whispered to Brenda.

'Probably one the kids have written themselves. They don't go a bundle on Oscar Wilde, Marlowe and Shakespeare. No relevance to them.'

Joe scowled. 'No relevance? It seems to me the kids these days are carrying just as many blades as Hamlet, Macbeth, and Julius Caesar's oppos.'

'They weren't Caesar's oppos,' Brenda corrected him. 'They stabbed him in the back.'

Joe grunted softly. 'A bit like you when I have to leave the café.'

Brenda never got the chance to respond. Martin brought the class to a close, and dismissed the students. As they filed out, one or two paused for a quick, quiet word, and once they had all left, he made his way to the back of the room and sat with Joe and Brenda. 'I don't have much time, I'm afraid. Is it about Sheila?'

The words were curt and clipped, yet he appeared friendly enough, but Joe mentally dismissed it as a front. Usually willing to give others the benefit of the doubt, Joe had already made up his mind about Martin. He was Marlon, he was Mervyn, he was a killer and he was a threat to their friend.

From Joe's prospective, almost everyone was tall, and Martin fell easily into that category. Little over six feet in height, slim and fit for his age, he had a good head of hair, which was getting a little thin at the crown. He was a good-looking man (Joe based the assumption on Brenda's more experienced opinion) with finely chiselled features and soft brown eyes, and on those occasions when Joe met him, he had always been a little reticent, almost timid, as if he were treading a careful path of uneven paving stones in an effort not to offend anyone.

But here, in the classroom, he was a different

man. Firmly in control, a genuine leader.

In response to Martin's query that they were here concerning Sheila, Joe replied, 'Not really. It's more about you, Mervyn Nellis and Marlon Newman.'

He was certain that the names registered, but Martin hid it well. 'Who?'

'Gar, don't come that with me. I know all about you, and so does Eliot Banks at North Shires.'

Brenda sighed. 'So much for diplomacy. Joe, you're about as tactful as a cruise missile.'

Martin leaned forward, elbows resting on his knees, hands clasped ahead of him, and he fixed Joe's eyes with a resigned gaze. 'I don't have a clue what you're talking about.'

Brenda opened her bag, and took out the photocopies Banks had given Joe. She handed them over to Martin and insisted, 'Are you saying those men are not you? Because from where I'm sat, you're the spitting image of them.'

Martin studied the grainy images on the photocopies, and spent a long time reading the text accompanying the newspaper stories. At length, he chuckled, and handed the photocopies back. 'You're right. I do look like them.' He sat back. 'But, unfortunately, I don't come from Darlington, and I don't think I've ever been anywhere near Ripon other than on the occasional day trip. I can understand your concern, especially after reading those stories and taking into account the way Sheila is, but you've got it completely wrong.'

Joe still did not believe him. 'I'll tell you

something that puzzles me, Martin. You've known Sheila for a year, you've been married, how long, three months now. According to her, she's asked you several times to join the 3rd Age Club, yet you have always refused.' He aimed an accusing finger at the photocopies as Brenda slotted them back into the file. 'You know about my reputation, and you didn't want us tumbling this little lot, did you?'

Martin sighed again. 'You know, you need a lot of tolerance to teach seventeen and eighteen-year-old kids, and they're experts in the art of winding you up. Frankly, Joe, you're doing a good impression of them, and you're beginning to tax my patience. Listen to me very carefully. I am not Marlon Nellis or Mervyn Newman—'

'Mervyn Nellis and Marlon Newman,' Joe interrupted.

'Whoever. I am neither of them. True, I'm a widower. My wife died some years ago. Natural causes, and she's buried in my home town of York. I'll point you to her grave, if you wish. I understand your concern for Sheila, but you have this all wrong. I am no threat to her, and I want to see her well again, every bit as much as you do. Now why don't you two go away before I reach breaking point?'

Joe stood up, and Brenda joined him.

'This doesn't end here,' Joe warned. 'I'll be having a word with Howard.'

'Then I hope he has more sense than you.'

Joe and Brenda left the building, made their way back into the icy cold, and climbed into his car.

'That didn't go well, did it?' Brenda observed.

'He's lying,' Joe assured. 'In his position, wouldn't you lie?'

'Probably, but he seemed so sure. Are you really going to see Howard?'

Joe tapped agitated fingers on the steering wheel, and then fired the engine. 'Difficult. He's Sheila's blood relative and it might be awkward for him to investigate. Gemma is probably a better bet. This is Sanford; her beat.' He thought about it for a moment. 'Tell you what, I'll see if I can get in touch with Maddy. She's a genealogist, and she'll know how to trace Martin's past. If anyone can find his wife's grave, it's her.'

'Yes and if she really is buried in York, then we've probably got it wrong.' Brenda harrumphed impotently at the inclement weather. 'You do know Martin will tell Sheila about our little tête à tête, don't you?'

'Yes, and we'll have to deal with the flak.'

It took twenty minutes to get back to The Lazy Luncheonette, only to find the place in a state of pandemonium, and a queue of customers rapidly losing patience. As Joe and Brenda entered through the back door to find no sign of Lee and one of Cheryl's friends, Pauline and Kayleigh, watching over the hot stoves, two women left the queue and walked out in a fit of temper.

'What the hell's going on?' Joe demanded.

Lee appeared from behind the counter. 'Oh, thank God you're back, Uncle Joe. It's the bar mitzvah machine. It's thrown a wobbler.'

'Bar mitzvah machine?'

'He means the barista, Joe.'

He did not need Brenda's translation. He hurried through the service counter and found the barista and adjacent area covered in what looked like curdled cream.

'What the hell—'

'It was my fault, Joe,' Cheryl interrupted. 'I left it to my friend Kayleigh, and she put cream instead of milk in it.' She blushed. 'Well, she thought it was cream. Actually, it was a raspberry flavoured yoghurt, and when she put it under the heater, it splattered everywhere.' She gestured around the rear of the counter where traces of the gunge could be seen across the walls and nearby tables.

'She put yoghurt in a coffeemaker?'

'Calm down, Joe,' Brenda advised.

'And not even normal yoghurt but raspberry flavoured.' Joe laid the evil eye on Cheryl. 'What was she trying to make? A yoghucccino? Did she not learn to read at school?' His fury building, he demanded, 'And where is she?'

'She went home. She was terrified of what you'd say.' Cheryl was humbly contrite. 'I'm sorry, Joe. We were trying to clean it up before you got back.'

'Then you'd better get on with it before—'

The woman at the front of the queue rapped on the counter. 'Oi. Are we gonna get any service here, or what?'

Joe turned a mock, sweet smile on her. 'Certainly, madam. What would like? A bacon and raspberry yoghurt sandwich? Or perhaps a tuna salad with yoghurt? If I pour orange juice over it, you can have three courses in one bun; starter, main meal and dessert.'

Pulling her tabard in place, Brenda pushed him out of the way and took over at the counter. She smiled at the customer. 'You'll have to forgive us, luv. It's been a trying morning.' From the side of her mouth, she said to Joe, 'You'd better keep an eye on lunches, Joe, while Lee and Cheryl get the mess cleared up.'

Chapter Seven

Immediately the lunchtime rush was out of the way, Joe grabbed a quick bite to eat, put on his coat, and with a brief explanation to Brenda, excused himself.

Working his way round the convoluted route which would bring him onto Doncaster Road heading into Sanford, he made mental plans for the afternoon. First on the agenda was a visit to Kimbolton Terrace, to speak to some of Billy Trelfus's neighbours.

As he battled the weight of traffic, he made a brief call to Maddy Chester, a genealogist with whom he had an on/off relationship, and she confirmed that she was in Australia with members of her family, and she would be there until after the New Year. As a consequence, Joe decided that once he was finished with the residents of Kimbolton Terrace, he would call at the police station and have a few words with Gemma on the subject of Martin Naylor.

He was not unduly concerned with the Bailey/Dixon/Trelfus affair. Gemma had no more evidence against Tel Bailey than she did against anyone else, and it was likely that the case would dry up and remain unsolved.

The same could not be said of the threat to Sheila, if indeed such a threat existed. But without Maddy's assistance, the police remained as his only hope of clearing or convicting Martin.

It was a path fraught with difficulties. As Brenda pointed out, Martin would undoubtedly speak to Sheila, and once Gemma was brought into the equation, she would inevitably tell Howard (they were, after all, living together) and as Sheila's only blood relative in the UK, he was bound to become involved, and at some stage, Peter Riley Jnr and his brother Aaron would be informed. Both of Sheila's sons lived in America, but Joe knew them well. They were fiercely protective of their mother, and he would not be surprised to learn that they were ready to jump on a flight to the UK and confront Martin.

And if it should prove that Martin was, indeed, innocent…

Still fighting with the traffic on Doncaster Road, winding his way towards the canal side streets, Joe shuddered at the prospect. Like it or not, the morning's visit to Sanford Park Comprehensive had fired the ignition, and set the lumbering gears of the machinery into motion. He would just have to live with whatever the consequences. But even as he worried about the outcome, he had no regrets. His overriding concern was the safety of a woman he had known for half a century.

Turning into Kimbolton Terrace, an almost exact duplicate of Tandy Street, Joe parked up, and left the engine running for a few minutes while he decided on his approach.

The door of number seventeen had a metal grille placed over it. Bailey and Dixon, he guessed. It was a standard, anti-burglar procedure for any house undergoing renovation. At number fifteen (Trelfus's place) next-door a similar grille had been put in place, but this was crisscrossed with police "scene of crime" tape.

But looking over the crime scene would do him any good. Whatever tales the empty house had to tell, they were the exclusive province of the police and their scientific support services.

He killed the engine, climbed out, locked up the car and crossed the street to number eleven, noticing (with some humour) that there was no number thirteen. Triskaidekaphobia; an extreme fear of the number thirteen which frequently manifested itself in the older streets of industrial towns like Sanford where the everyday, working people of days gone by were swamped in superstition.

He knocked on the door, and presently a forty-something woman answered. 'We don't want none.'

Joe's irritation flashed before he could control it. 'How do you know? I might be selling English lessons.'

The lady of the house, an overweight bottle blonde dressed in scruffy, rip-knee jeans and a thin, flowery top which showed her bra, made to close the door, but Joe stopped her.

'No. Please. I'm sorry. I'm not selling anything. I'm here about the old boy at number fifteen.'

Suspicion still haunting her pudgy face, she opened the door again. 'You're too short to be a copper, so are you a reporter?'

'No. I'm a private investigator, and I've been asked to do some poking around.'

She relaxed a moment and shuffled her furry mules on the doormat. 'Well, what do you wanna know? Come on, it's perishing standing here.'

'Someone told me that you get a lot of builders and such knocking on your doors, trying to get you to sell up.'

She nodded. 'They're a pain in the butt. Every day they come knocking. I wouldn't care, but I don't even own this place. I'm only the tenant. I just tell 'em to p—'

'Yeah. I can imagine,' Joe interrupted. 'How well did you know old Trelfus?'

'Too well. He was a miserable old twonk. Always moaning, whingeing, especially when we have the telly on. I meanersay, we has to have the volume turned up on account of my old man's nearly deaf.'

'Did you know about the argument he had with the builder the other day?'

'Half the bloody street knew about it. Old Billy was shouting the odds, and the young lad, him as what killed the old git, went round and gave him short shrift.'

'So did you see Tel on the night Trelfus died?'

'Yes. He turned up roaring drunk about half past eleven. Had some young tart with him. I don't know how much she charges, but the state he was in, she wouldn't have had to do much for it.'

Joe put her biased opinions to one side. 'But they went into number seventeen, not Trelfus's place. Right?' She nodded and Joe went on, 'So you didn't hear the argument when Trelfus was killed?'

For the first time the woman seemed hazy. 'Not really. We heard something going on, but we was busy with other matters at the time, me and my other half. And don't ask what we were doing. It's nowt to do with you.'

Joe's mind ran along automatic tracks, and he shuddered at the prospect of this woman in the throes of sexual excess. 'So who called the cops?'

She shrugged. 'Haven't a clue. Wasn't me. Probably one of the nosy buggers across the street.'

She went to close the door again, but Joe stopped her. 'Sorry, missus, just another couple of things and I'll leave you in peace. You get builders round here every day, and Tel Bailey says that him and his partner, Denny Dixon, have done a bit of door-knocking here. Can you point me to any other builders, estate agents and the like who come round regular?'

She gave the matter a moment's thought. 'There's two that I can think of. One's a builder. Parson's nose, or something, he calls himself. Sleazy toe rag. Beard. Usually has a big bruiser with him. The other is a red-haired woman. Gotta be sixty if she's a day. Mutton dressed as lamb, that one. Works for some estate agents who auction houses off. Her and that builder I mentioned are round here every other day. Proper nuisances, they are.'

The information confirmed Joe's suspicions. He needed to speak to Iain Parsloe and Archie

Hepple's wife, Frankie.

He thanked the woman, made his way back to his car, took a couple of shunts to turn it round, and drove out of Kimbolton, heading towards the auction house on Pontefract Road, but when he got there, it was to learn that the Hepples were in the middle of a general auction. If he waited, it would mean a delay of at least a couple of hours. He doubled back, made his way through the streets, fighting once again with pre-Christmas traffic, one eye on the clock – he had to be home early to get ready for Churchill's – he eventually pulled up outside Parsloe's yard.

It was no different to Bailey and Dixon's place a couple of miles away. Bags of cement stored under a tarpaulin, various bits and pieces of scaffolding, planking, and other timber strewn about the place, occasional warning signs in various colours propped up against the surrounding barbed wire-topped fences, and a tiny office in a Portakabin to one side.

When he stepped in, Parsloe was on the telephone, but the conversation told Joe that he was speaking to his bookie, and not a customer. Almost immediately, he put the phone down. 'What can I do you for, squire?'

'You could tell me about Billy Trelfus at Kimbolton Terrace,' Joe announced.

Parsloe's features darkened immediately. 'If I were you, I'd clear off. While you can still walk.'

Joe ignored the threat. 'Y'see, this is the kind of crap I get most of the time, and it doesn't persuade me. A couple of days ago, someone topped old Trelfus, and Tel Bailey is in the frame for it. Now I know Tel. A scrapper, sure, but no way is he a killer, and according to him and Denny Dixon, they haven't been hassling the residents of Kimbolton for months. But you're round there every other day.'

Footsteps sounded behind Joe. He turned to find himself confronted with a tall, muscular man, sporting a similar beard to Parsloe. Narrowed eyes homed in on Joe, and the lips turned downwards in a scowl of menace.

'Bob, why don't you show this clown out?' Parsloe turned his attention to Joe. 'Sod off, and don't come back. Not if you know what's good for you.'

Despite all that could be said of Joe, good and bad, he was not stupid. Against this obviously aggressive thug, he would have no chance. He glowered at Parsloe. 'I'll be back. And next time I won't be on my own, so you'd better try and find some of that Christmas peace and goodwill everyone else is looking for.'

He was determined not to hurry, but the slightest movement from the minder, Bob, prompted him to rethink, and he rushed from the cabin, back out into the street, and climbed into his car. And for once, he locked the doors behind him.

He was boiling mad, mostly with himself and his impotence in the face of such intimidation. He had been like it all his life. Aggressive, outspoken, but absolutely useless in a fight, and he remained uncertain how to handle the present situation. A complaint to the police would get him nowhere.

Gemma had already warned him to keep out of the business. And yet, it was obvious that assuming Parsloe wasn't suffering anything more than a bad mood, the man had something he would prefer not to talk about, and Joe wanted to know what.

He started the engine, made his way slowly back into town, leaving his car, once again, in the multi-storey car park attached to the Galleries mall, from where he crossed Gale Street, and after a few minutes of negotiation with Constable Noel Wickes on the front desk, sat with Gemma, who suppressed her annoyance when she learned that he was not here to interfere in the Trelfus inquiry. She listened carefully to what he had to say, and over a cup of tea, studied the North Shires file.

'I have to say, I don't remember either of these incidents, but then again, Darlington doesn't come under our division, and Ripon is North Yorkshire, not West. But it's all a bit hazy, Joe. The two men in these photographs do look like Martin but that doesn't mean anything. George Robson looks like one of the actors from that American comedy series from years ago; *Cheers*. You remember it?' Gemma waited for Joe to agree with a curt nod. 'But I don't see many people asking for George's autograph. And according to this report, Deirdre Ullsworth died from atropine poisoning. Sheila doesn't have any of the major symptoms associated with atropine.'

'Nausea, vomiting, diarrhoea? All right, so those are only a few of the symptoms. The way I see it is leopards might not be able to change their spots, but they can adapt their hunting techniques.'

She agreed immediately. 'I understand where you're coming from, but I have to take a broader view. If Martin really is poisoning her, it would show up in the hospital tests, and according to my best information, they've proved nothing. According to what Howard told me, the doctors reckon her problem is psychological, not physical.'

'A nice little theory to hang something on when they don't know what's wrong.' Joe puffed out his breath. 'Are you telling me you won't look into this?'

'It's not that simple. I need to take advice on what we can and can't do. You're accusing a man based on a resemblance to the two men wanted in connection with the previous incidents. That and the fact that his wife is unwell.' Gemma got to her feet, and moved round the tiny office to her photocopier, where she began to copy the documents. As she waited for them to arrive in the tray, she went on, 'I'll have a word with Don Oughton, and see what he has to say. I'll also speak to Howard when he gets home tonight, but you do know this is likely to stir up a hornet's nest between you and Sheila.'

Joe shrugged, took out his tobacco tin and began to roll a cigarette. 'What am I supposed to do? Wait until we're lowering her coffin into the ground, and then accuse him?'

'I don't know. But I do know you can't smoke that in here.'

'I'm not going to, I'm not going to. It's for when I get outside.'

Gemma handed his file back and collected the

copies. 'Leave it with me, Joe. I promise I'll get onto the Chief Super as soon as.'

He came out of the police station with the feeling that he was making no progress, or if he was, it was in reverse, and with the time coming up to half past three, he had no idea what to do next, so he climbed into his car, lit the cigarette, and joined the afternoon throng for the journey back to The Lazy Luncheonette.

It was little short of a nightmare. The Salvation Army band were playing a series of Christmas carols on the corner of Gale Street and Market Square, the sound grating on Joe's nerves, and stuck in traffic, he could not avoid it other than turning on the radio, which poured forth more Christmas jingles.

As an adult, he had never been a big lover of Christmas; something which he diagnosed as symptomatic of his solitary lifestyle. Even in the decade when he was married to Alison, he had never made a big fuss over the Yuletide season. Young Danny had made a slight difference to his approach, but that, he recognised, was only the tendency towards indulgence when it came to children, which in turn was a factor of his lack of same. Beyond that, he could live without the cloying schmaltz of Christmas and New Year. He rarely switched the television on at any time during the year, but it was off even longer during the season of (theoretical) goodwill, and he spent much of his time alone, surfing the web, looking for holiday locations, or attending to the administrative needs of The Lazy Luncheonette and the 3rd Age Club.

The crew of The Lazy Luncheonette made an effort to decorate the place in the run-up to Christmas. A small tree stood to one side, it's lights flashing, fake presents stacked under it, more fairy lights strung around the counter, tinsel adorning the walls, and one or two posters wishing patrons a Merry Christmas. None of it had Joe's approval, but it was entirely in keeping with his hands-off management style of the café, that no one sought his permission or approbation. While behind the counter, he was as surly and irritable as at any other time of year.

Leaving the town centre behind, picking up the dual carriageway of Doncaster Road, he came to the conclusion that it was the way he was, there was nothing to be done about it. If he had to grin and bear Christmas, then Christmas would have to grin and bear his Scrooge-esque tetchiness.

When he got back to the café, he found them in mufti, ready for closing down. Kayleigh, the errant, casual assistant who had fed yoghurt into the barista sat with Brenda, Cheryl and her other friend, Pauline, while Lee was in the kitchen, making sure everything was closed down for the night.

Joe approved. Lee might not be the sharpest tool in the box, but he had learned his lessons well over the years, and he knew the shut-down routine. All cooking and heating appliances had to be switched off, the fridge, freezer and chillers must be properly secured and running at the appropriate temperatures to ensure that no fresh foods deteriorated. Amongst his final tasks was a brief check of stocks, ensuring they had ample supplies for the following day.

As Joe entered and poured himself a cup of tea, Lee presented him with a short list: mince pies, cream cakes, vanilla ice cream, and at the bottom of the list, flavoured yoghurts. When he read it, Joe cast a scowl at Kayleigh.

'I'm really sorry, Mr Murray.'

'You're also banned from using the barista,' he told her. 'But we'll let it pass this time. Consider it my contributing to the Christmas spirit, and stick to delivering meals and pouring tea in future.' He switched his attention to Lee. 'I might need your help tomorrow, Lee.'

His giant nephew frowned. 'I weren't thinking of taking the day off, Uncle Joe.'

Taking a swallow of tea, Joe shook his head and sighed. 'I didn't mean I need your help here. I mean out there.' He jerked a thumb over his shoulder, indicating the dark streets beyond The Lazy Luncheonette's entrance. 'I've had a bit of hassle this afternoon, and I might need you to persuade people to back off.'

He grinned in anticipation. He smacked a giant fist into his opposite palm. 'Let me at 'em. I'll make 'em spill the sprouts.'

Brenda frowned. 'You mean you'll make them talk? Spill the beans?'

'Yeah, but it's Christmas. We don't have beans at Christmas. We have sprouts.'

Chapter Eight

For most STAC outings, Sanford Coach Services provided transport, but most STAC outings were to other towns and cities. With Churchill's less than two miles from the town centre, the club members made their own way there, some driving, most, like Joe, arriving by taxi.

Joe had ordered his cab to collect Brenda on the way. Since neither of them were attached or had escorts for the evening, they had decided to share a table... hopefully with Sheila and Martin. When he got to Brenda's place, she was ready. Grandly dressed in a dark, sober jacket and pants which offset the gold glittering around her neck and on her fingers, she was a perfect match for Joe's dark suit, white shirt and black bow tie

'Normally, I'd expect Sheila and Martin to join us,' Brenda said, unconsciously echoing Joe's thoughts. 'But after this morning, even if she makes it, I think she'll avoid us.'

'Other than having a few words to say,' Joe responded gloomily as the cab wove its way through the streets to join Wakefield Road.

Standing close to the motorway junction, the restaurant/nightspot sported a huge, neon sign in the shape of the wartime Prime Minister, complete with bowler hat and cigar, shining through the night, and below it was a Christmas tree, its fairy lights flashing in the cold night. And yet, notwithstanding its brash exterior, quality was assured. Churchill's official rating was four star but throughout Sanford it was known as the finest quality restaurant; *the* place to hold a celebration dinner.

Paying the taxi and getting out, Joe found a good number of their fellow members already making their way in.

The club chairman, at least for the time being, Captain Les Tanner was ahead of them in the queue. A former part-time soldier, he looked militarily precise in his regimental blazer and tie, and hanging on Tanner's arm was his long-time lady love, Sylvia Goodson, looking equally regal in a flowing gown and faux fox fur wrap. Despite her easy-going, contingent demeanour, Sylvia was a vociferous campaigner in the fight against cruelty to animals, amongst which she numbered fox-hunting and animals bred purely for their skins.

As always Joe felt slightly uncomfortable in his finery, but he soon relaxed once they were in the main lounge and a waiter showed them to a discreet table for two off to one side of the dining area.

Most tables, he noticed, seated four, facing a small stage and dance floor. On the podium, a quartet of musicians was setting up their stands.

'The Ronaldo Lombardy Combo,' Brenda said with a hearty chuckle. 'Ronnie Lund and his pals.'

'He was part of the Sanford Colliery Brass Band before the pit shut down, you know. Not bad on the horn, but hardly Royal Albert Hall fodder.'

Across the aisle from them, making up a

foursome, were George Robson, Owen Frickley and the Staineses, Alec and Julia. All four greeted them cheerily, and asked after Sheila. Both Joe and Brenda told what they knew about her state of health, but did not mention the more disconcerting news of the past twenty-four hours.

Further along was Stewart Dalmer sat with a woman Joe did not know. A tall, rangy man who had been a member of the club for about three years, he was a former tutor at Sanford Technical College. After their intimacy in Cornwall, Dalmer had invited Brenda as his partner for the evening, but she turned him down, preferring Joe's company instead – a situation which gave Joe a good feeling, but which had the opposite effect on Dalmer, judging by the occasional dark glances he cast at them.

The disastrous week in Hayle following Sheila's wedding to Martin, had been one of the most pivotal weeks in Joe's life. He had come within a hair's breadth of abandoning not only the club and his friends, but Sanford altogether. Brenda, it was, who had helped open his eyes, and brought about a change of heart. Tanner was due to step down as chairman in the New Year, and Joe would go head-to-head with Dalmer in the ensuing election. According to George Robson, Joe was odds-on favourite to win the seat he had given up when Denise Latham was killed. He had technically relinquished his administrative duties attached to the club when he resigned the Chair, but some were left in his hands, even though he was no longer an officer, thanks largely to his negotiating skills, and he was actively looking forward to his re-election in January.

But even as he thought of it, another problem reared its hypothetical head. Ever since the club's inception, Joe had been chairman, Brenda the treasurer, and Sheila the secretary. Indeed, the 3rd Age Club had been Brenda and Sheila's idea. With the potential for internal conflict raised by the revelations of the last twenty-four hours, would they be able to work together as a team?

And it was not only the club, he ruminated as the waiter brought their first course (fruit juice for Joe, mulligatawny soup for Brenda). How could they continue working together at The Lazy Luncheonette? As he sipped tentatively at his freshly squeezed orange juice, he began to wish he had never heard of Eliot Banks, North Shires Insurance, and he certainly wished Sheila had never met Martin Naylor, let alone married him.

Brenda was still only halfway through her soup when, much to their surprise, Martin and Sheila joined them.

He was classically dressed in a dinner suit, frilled dress shirt, complete with cummerbund and bow tie, while Sheila wore a formal evening gown in dark ruby, which, like Brenda's outfit, was speckled with items of jewellery.

Joe and Brenda were speechless, neither of them able to think of anything to say. Sheila greeted them with a severe smile, Martin with a poker-face nod, and the pair took their seats.

'I assumed you kept the seats vacant for Martin and me,' Sheila said.

Joe still could not speak and it was left to Brenda to respond. 'I, er, well, yes. Of course. We weren't sure whether you'd be here.'

Sheila's smile was more pointed. 'After your conversation with Martin this morning, I decided I should make the effort.'

That was enough for Joe. In anticipation of what was to come, he gulped down the remainder of his fruit juice, and got to his feet. 'I'm going outside for a smoke.'

'Between courses, Joe?' Sheila said.

'Between battles,' he retorted, and marched away.

Churchill's was not possessed of a smoke area, and he had no alternative but to step out through the front doors, ensuring he had his ticket stub with him so he could get back in. Ignoring the bitter cold, he took a cigarette case from his pocket, in which were a dozen, previously rolled cigarettes. Putting one between his lips, he lit it, drew the smoke in, and let it out with jittery hiss.

If he had been surprised by their arrival, he was not remotely put out when Martin joined him. If there was to be an argument, let it be between him Sheila's husband. He was better arguing with men than women… especially women like Sheila.

Martin smiled down upon him. 'I had fruit juice, same as you. Knocked it back in one hit.' His smile faded 'What did you think, Joe? Did you really imagine I wouldn't mention it to her?'

'No. I knew you would. But it changes nothing. All right, all right, so you claim we've got it wrong. Fine. You'll excuse me if I choose not to believe that until I have some kind of proof. As far as I'm concerned, you are Mervyn Nellis and Marlon Newman, and in that case, Sheila's life is under threat.'

Martin laughed. Joe imagined it was supposed to be a good-natured chuckle, but it came out as something more sinister. 'Conspiracy theories. I deal with them all the time. Whenever anything goes wrong for the kids, they haven't done their homework, haven't taken in the lessons I'm delivering, failed a crucial test, it's always some kind of conspiracy to hold them back. It never seems to dawn on them that it's their own fault. I'm listening to you and it reminds me of them. You're a good detective, Joe. Your reputation is county-wide, and even further afield if your friends in the 3rd Age Club are to be believed. But you're like all the rest of us. A long way from perfect. And this time, you're so far off the mark that you've almost turned the bullets on yourself.'

Joe took another drag on his cigarette and watched the wind whip the smoke away into the night. 'Do you understand the principle of friendship?'

Martin frowned. 'I think so.'

'I don't think you do. I'm not talking about colleagues, I'm not talking about drinking buddies, I'm talking about true, genuine friends, people you've known for most of your life. Sheila comes under that heading. We were kids in the schoolyard together, me, her, and Brenda. Think about the kids you teach, think about the young lad waiting on us tonight. We've been friends for longer than those kids have been on this Earth. And when you've thought about that, ask yourself a question. What kind of a friend would I be if I didn't look out for her welfare?' He drew on the cigarette again. 'And I'll tell you something else. If Sheila chooses to bawl me out over it, it'll change nothing. Until I have some proof that you are no threat to her, I'll carry on sticking my nose in.'

He dropped the cigarette on the floor, crushed it under the soles of his highly-polished shoes, turned on his heels, and marched back into the restaurant.

* * *

Inside, a similar debate was taking place between Sheila and Brenda, but where Joe and Martin had held their tempers, the two women were on the verge of losing theirs.

'How dare you make such allegations?' Sheila demanded. Like her husband, she had opted for fruit juice and drank it in one gulp, and the young, embarrassed waiter hovered nearby, waiting to clear away the detritus of the first course.

'Not with any pleasure, and not without some evidence.' Brenda's tough tones turned more cynical. 'Unfortunately, this is a dinner and dance, and we didn't bring the evidence with us.'

'Evidence? You mean the photocopied rubbish you showed Martin this morning? He told me about it, and he also told me where to find his first wife's grave in York, which is good enough for me. Whoever is in those files, it's not him.'

'You can't say that because you haven't seen them. And it's all very well him telling you where to find a grave, are you absolutely certain about it? Has he shown you the death certificate? And even if he is telling it like it was, how do you know it's the absolute truth? He could have had a string of women between that first wife and you. For God's sake, Sheila, Joe and I are concerned for you.'

'And that,' Sheila retorted jabbing her finger into the table, 'is the only reason I'm willing to put the matter behind us.'

'Well we're not,' Joe said as he returned and sat alongside Brenda. His eyes burned into Sheila. 'When I know Martin is innocent, and I mean *know* not suspect, then I'll back off and apologise. Until then, I'll do what I always do, keep pushing my oar in.'

Martin re-joined them as Sheila returned Joe's fiery gaze. 'Have you remembered who fought on your behalf when you were suspected of murder? Not once but twice? I argued for you, Joe Murray, because I believed in your innocence. And according to the grapevine, you're fighting for young Terry Bailey because you believe he's innocent. Wouldn't it be more in keeping with that attitude if you were fighting for Martin's innocence?'

'If I was convinced of it, yes. But I'm not. I don't want our Gemma coming knocking on my door telling me you've been found dead and he's done a runner.' Joe pointed an angry finger at Martin.

'If I could just get a word in,' the man himself said, 'we're providing a wonderful spectacle for everyone else.'

They all looked around, and realised the accuracy of his observation. The argument could be heard on the nearby tables, and all eyes were upon them. As they looked across, Les Tanner got to his feet and crossed the aisle to stand alongside their table.

'Forgive me, Sheila, Brenda, Joe, Martin, but there's obviously some friction between you. Whatever it is, may I suggest you put it to one side. This is hardly the time and place for such a battle, and all you're doing is providing spectator sport for everyone else.'

Whenever Tanner had anything to say, Joe could always be guaranteed to come up with a reply, but for once he was speechless. Brenda, too, remained quiet, Martin gave Tanner an obsequious smile of apology, but Sheila was unrepentant.

'I will not sit here and have my husband accused of crimes he has not committed.' On the phrase "accused of crimes" she pointed a finger at Joe and Brenda.

Tanner was equal to her. 'Then may I suggest, Sheila, that you move to another table.' He smiled gruffly at the young waiter, still waiting to serve them. 'I'm sure this young man can accommodate you.'

Brenda rose to the suggestion. 'I think that's an excellent solution, Les. Thank you. But don't you move, Sheila. Given your poor health, Joe and I will oblige by shifting elsewhere.'

For Joe it was his worst nightmare materialised. The very situation he had been afraid of had come to pass, and it was with a feeling of deep regret that he allowed the maitre d' to show them to another table, adjacent to the one occupied by the Pyecocks, and Mort Norris and his wife.

'Well,' Joe said as they settled in and waited for another attendant to deliver the main course, 'that's raddled the night good and proper, hasn't it?'

'Be honest, Joe. We were expecting it, weren't we? We know Sheila, we know what she's like. You're the guy who doesn't shy away from awkward questions, and I can be hard. But neither of us is a patch on her.' As the meal arrived, she picked up a knife and fork and tackled the traditional roast turkey dinner with gusto. 'The only thing is,' she muttered through a mouthful of roast potato, 'if Martin really is innocent, we'll have to beg for forgiveness.'

'And it'll be slow coming.'

As the meal came to an end, the Ronaldo Lombardy Combo, a four-piece band consisting of trombone/saxophone, guitar, keyboard, drums, went into action, opening with an instrumental version of *Winter Wonderland*. People were slow to take to the dance floor, but eventually, with Les Tanner and Sylvia, Alec and Julia Staines leading the way, the floor began to fill up.

With the lack of originality for which the band was best known, they followed up with a variety of Christmas/Winter numbers, most of them instrumental, but with the guitarist – a portly man named Stan Ewell, whom Joe knew slightly – performing the occasional vocal.

Joe and Brenda danced a couple of times, and by quarter past eleven, putting aside the argument with Sheila and Martin, Joe declared the evening a pleasant one.

He and Brenda climbed into the taxi, Joe instructed the driver to take them to her bungalow.

'What are you doing about Martin?' Brenda asked as the driver turned right out of Churchill's, heading towards the town centre.

'It's out of my hands,' he replied. 'Gemma has all the information, and she's promised to look into it. More than that, she'll be talking to Howard about it. In the meantime, whether she likes it or not, we have to keep an eye on Sheila. If she gets worse, we need to press the medics and the cops.'

Ten minutes after leaving Churchill's, the driver stopped outside Brenda's place.

'Come in for coffee.'

He glanced at his watch. 'I dunno. It's getting late.'

'Come on, Joe. I don't wanna be on my own tonight. Not after the argument with Sheila.'

He resigned himself to the inevitable, and paid off the driver. 'I can see where this will lead.'

Brenda smiled slyly. 'If you're lucky, it will.'

Chapter Nine

Joe's inbuilt alarm woke him automatically just after five o'clock the following morning, and for a moment, he had to wonder where he was.

This was not the scantily furnished bedroom of his council flat, and it certainly wasn't any bedroom in Tandy Street. He had not been so drunk the previous night to know that he hadn't moved in to his incomplete new home yet. So where...

The woman alongside him stirred, turning over and throwing an arm around him, and his memory clicked into place. A night with Brenda was the perfect way to end what had been an excellent evening (the argument with Sheila and Martin aside) and although he was still tired, he was ready to face the trials and tribulations of the day ahead. First on the agenda – after serving breakfast to the ever-hungry drivers of Sanford Brewery – would be a call to Gemma, and then a second call, this time to Howard. After lunch, when things were winding down, it would be another call, in this case, physical, to Ian Parsloe, but he would not make the mistake of going alone. And if things went according to plan, he should still have time to call on Archie Hepple and speak to his wife, Frankie.

He showered and shaved in Brenda's bathroom, while the woman herself dragged her weary bones from the bed, and as he studied his wrinkled face in the mirror, questions formed in his mind, the principal amongst which was why Brenda would keep a razor and shaving brush in the bathroom. He decided it was best not to ask, and instead concentrated his fine mind on the problem of Martin and Sheila.

Despite their best friend's determined defence of her new husband, Joe was not prepared to let the matter drop without definitive proof that Martin Naylor was not Mervyn Nellis and/or Marlon Newman.

After making a quick call to Lee, instructing him to open up The Lazy Luncheonette, he and Brenda left her house a little after six o'clock, and she drove to his place or Leeds Road, where he changed into his working clothes, picked up his car, and followed her to the café.

A fine but icy December drizzle left the pavements and roads treacherous, and gritter lorries could be seen here and there, spreading sand and salt on the tarmac. Parking at the rear of Britannia Parade, they were glad to get in, out of the cold and in the cocoon of warmth in the kitchen where Lee already had breakfast preparations under control.

There was only one person in the dining area, a trucker heading home to either Norwich or Northwich – Lee could not remember which – who had been parked in the lane behind the café overnight, and by the time the first of the Sanford Brewery draymen arrived, at seven fifteen, Joe was in full battle readiness.

With his typical, surly rejoinders he dealt with

the apparently never-ending queue quickly and efficiently. Cheryl delivered the meals and put up with a lot more suggestive chat than Sheila would have ever tolerated. She laughed it off as good-natured banter, although Joe noticed that it drew one or two irritated glances from his nephew.

'Don't worry about it, lad,' he advised. 'Your wife's more than capable of dealing with these bananas.'

By half past nine, with the rush from the offices above them over and done with, Joe was ready to go into his day's plan, when Howard walked in.

'I'm not currying any favours with my boss, Joe,' he admitted as he took a cup of tea from Brenda, who joined them. 'I called on Aunt Sheila on my way here, and she told me about last night's argument. Gemma also told me the rest of the tale last night, so I'm fairly well clued up on it.'

'We're sorry for dragging you into it, Howard,' Brenda admitted.

'Don't be. Even if this man, this Nellis or Newman or whatever he wants to call himself, proves not to be Martin, you did the right thing. Gemma will pull him in later today for interview. That makes it official, and the order came from Chief Superintendent Oughton, here in Sanford. Ray Dockerty, my immediate boss, is in complete agreement, but he ordered me to keep my distance because Sheila is my aunt. And according to the woman herself, things are bad between the three of you.'

'As bad as I can ever remember,' Joe said.

'No kidding, we've fallen out a good few times over the years, but never as bad as this.' He spread his hands apart in a gesture of appeal. 'What are we supposed to do? If he's some kind of serial poisoner, we can't leave Sheila at his mercy.'

Howard hastened to reassure him. 'I'm in your corner. Nellis has escaped justice for the last twelve years, and if it all comes to nothing, it won't be for the want of trying, and Sheila should be grateful for your efforts.'

Brenda chuckled. 'I can't see it, can you?' She put on a more serious face. 'Mind you, I can also see her point of view. She's invested everything in Martin, including herself, and in her position, I'd probably fight his corner, too.'

'I'll do my best to smooth the waters when it's over,' Howard promised. 'Either way, you're all going to need help to repair the divide between you.'

The debate would probably have gone on, but for the arrival of a familiar face: the man who had intimidated Joe at Parsloe's yard the previous day.

Joe scowled at him. 'What do you want?'

'Looking for Joe Murray?'

'That's me.'

Bob – the only name Joe knew him by – smiled evilly down. 'Well that's a turn up for the book, ain't it?'

Feeling a good deal more courageous than the previous day, Joe demanded, 'What do you want? That's twice I've asked you.'

'I'm authorised to offer you seventy-five thousand pounds in cash for number twenty-three

Tandy Street.'

Joe shook his head. 'It's not for sale. Goodbye.'

Bob sat down adjacent to Howard as if Joe had said nothing. 'You don't understand, Murray. We want that house. And it's very silly leaving it empty, especially while Tel Bailey's looking at a long stretch in the nick.' He spread his large hands before him. 'I mean, it'd be awful if something happened, wouldn't it?'

Joe put his cup down. 'It sounds to me, Mr…?'

'Kimberry. Bob Kimberry.'

'It sounds to me, Mr Kimberry, as if you're threatening me.'

Kimberry smiled. 'Nothing of the kind. I'm just here to give you a bit of friendly advice, that's all. We want that property.'

'All right. Can I give you a bit of friendly advice?' Joe did not wait for an answer. 'I'm only a little fella. Barely five foot six—'

'And that's only when he's wearing his trainers with the thick soles,' Brenda commented, with a sour glare on the newcomer.

'Thanks for nothing, Brenda.' Joe swung his focus back to Kimberry. 'I'm no good in a fight. Never have been. And you're about half my age. I'd have no chance. That's why I always need help, and it's why I backed away yesterday. I had no one with me. This time I have a couple of people to back me up.' He called over his shoulder, 'Lee, get out here.' He concentrated on Kimberry again. 'The gentleman sat next to you is

Detective Inspector Howard Riley of West Yorkshire CID. You might not have heard of him because he works in Leeds, but he's in a steady relationship with my niece, and if you're from Sanford, I'm sure you've heard of her. Detective Inspector Gemma Craddock.'

Kimberry's face paled as Lee lumbered from the kitchen, and stood alongside the table. 'What do you want, Uncle Joe?'

Joe maintained his focus on Kimberry. 'As if that's not enough, this lad is my nephew, as you might have guessed from the way he called me Uncle Joe. Lee Murray. He's a junior partner in this business, and at one time, he was a prop for the Sanford Bulls.' Joe's intense eyes homed in on Kimberry's widening pupils. 'He was tearing bigger blokes than you when he was in his teens.' He watched with satisfaction as the other man's face underwent a series of rapid changes, from confident threatening to worry, to out and out anxiety. Joe put a deliberate, hard edge into his voice. 'Do yourself a favour, Kimberry, and get out while you can.'

Kimberry got to his feet. 'You could regret this.'

For the first time, Howard spoke up. 'He'd better not. The house you're talking about, Kimberry, belonged to my late mother, and if anything should happen to it, you're the first person I'll come looking for.'

Confident in his control of the situation, Joe said, 'I'll tell you what I'll do with you. Parsloe wants the house, and he can have it. A hundred and fifty thousand, as is, with work still to be done on it.' He grinned at Howard. 'We can split the profit between us.'

Kimberry scowled. 'Shove it.'

Lee stood up and towered over Kimberry. 'Want me to slap him about, Uncle Joe? Or make mince pies of him.'

'You mean mincemeat, Lee,' Brenda suggested.

'Yeah, but it's Christmas, innit? And I like mince pies.'

Kimberry turned and marched out of the café, Joe concentrated on Howard, who said, 'Let me know if you get any more trouble with him, Joe.'

'You know him?'

'Vaguely. Remember, I'm still a comparative stranger in Sanford, but I'm sure I've heard Gemma talk about him. And the man he works for, the one you just mentioned, Parsley, or something like that.'

'Ian Parsloe? He's one of Bailey and Dixon's competitors. And like Bailey and Dixon, he's a nobody.'

'Just let me know if you get any more hassle. In the meantime, I'll pass it on to Gemma. A visit from her might just make them back off.' Howard checked his watch. 'I'd better get going, or I'm gonna be in trouble. Oh, while I think on. Gemma said, if you turn up at Gale Street this afternoon, you can sit in the observation room while she questions Martin Naylor.'

Joe grinned. 'Thanks, Howard. Hey, and don't be a stranger over Christmas. My door's always open to you.'

With Howard gone, Joe revised his initial plans. He needed to give Kimberry sufficient time to report to Parsloe. Instead, he left Brenda, Lee, Cheryl and her two friends to look after the café, climbed into his car, and drove across town, fighting yet again with the increasing traffic determined to clog the town centre, to the auction house belonging to the Hepple family.

It was little better than a long, ramshackle shed set in a small industrial plot on the north side of town, and with no more sales this side of the New Year, they were busy stocktaking when Ros let Joe in.

Archie was pleased to see him. A slim, rakish man, about sixty years of age, he was a member of the 3rd Age Club, but Joe could not remember the last time he had seen him or his wife in any of the discos or club meetings.

'Too busy, Joe. Wife and child still to feed, and that Ros absolutely refuses to find a husband. She'd rather pass the time faffing around with that waster, Bailey.'

'Yes, well, as it happens, it's Tel Bailey I've come to see you about. Not you in particular, but Ros, and while I'm here, I'd like a word with your missus. If you don't mind.' Joe added the final rider knowing full well that Archie would not object.

'Another one who costs me a fortune.' Archie grinned. 'Be my guest.'

He pulled Ros off to one side, she supplied him with a beaker of tea, and they sat together at an old, roll-top bureau, its flat surface pulled down allowing them somewhere to rest their drinks.

A slim woman, about thirty years of age, smartly, fashionably dressed in a chunky sweater and slim-fit jeans, there was a hard edge about her fine-boned features. She kept her dark hair short, enhancing the impression of a woman who knew her own mind, and as far as Joe was concerned, the only attraction was her eyes, baby blue pupils set in saucers of misty, milky white, which, when coupled to a pout on her ruby lips, were full of promise.

'You wanna know about the other night, don't you?' she asked, and Joe nodded. 'Yeah, the cops were asking too.' She shrugged her slender shoulders. 'I don't know what I can tell you, Joe. Tel asked me to meet him for a few beers in the Boat & Horses. There was football on the telly, and it turned into a session, didn't it? By closing time, he was smashed out of his brains, and what should have been a promising night turned into a disaster. He was too drunk to drive home, and I'd arrived by taxi, so we went round to Kimbolton Terrace.' She sighed. 'I only went with him because he was feeling a bit, er, anxious, if you get my meaning.'

Joe nodded his understanding. 'But he was too drunk?'

She sighed again. 'We got into the place, I fired up the camping stove to make a brew, and the next thing I knew, he was flat out on a sleeping bag, snoring his head off. I rang Frankie, asked her to pick me up, and sat it out while she turned up.'

'And you didn't hear anything from the old man next door?'

'Odd noises, yeah, but nothing that sounded like a barney. I'll tell you what I told the cops. Tel was in no state to go round there and get into a fight with him. I know Tel is a scrapper, but that night, Billy Trelfus would've won. That's how drunk Tel was.'

'How long were you waiting for Frankie?'

She shrugged again. 'Twenty minutes. Half an hour.'

'Long time.'

'Come on, Joe, she was in bed when I rang. She had to get dressed and everything.'

'Yeah. Okay. Thanks, Ros. I don't know how much further it'll get the cops, or whether it'll get Tel off the hook, but I promised our Gemma I'd pass on anything I came across.'

'Sorry, Joe. Can't tell you any more than that.'

'No worries. I need a word with your mother now, and I'll be out of your way.'

Ros's eyes narrowed. 'She's not my mother. She's my stepmother. My mother ran out on us, if you remember.'

Joe held up his hands in surrender. 'Apologies. I remember the scuttlebutt at the time.'

Ros wandered off, and Frankie took her place.

It was obvious that she was not the younger woman's natural mother. About Joe's height, a couple of years older than him, she was a classy, flame-haired, busty woman who had a tendency to wear skirts which were a little too short (in Joe's opinion) for her age, and she had a more agreeable attitude than her stepdaughter. Sitting opposite him, she crossed her knees, giving him a distracting and tempting view of the strong thighs.

'*Et maintenant*, Mr Murray. What can I do for you?'

Her accent was pure Yorkshire with a slight burr, and she had a habit of throwing in occasional French phrases, reminiscent of the character Del Boy in the TV comedy, *Only Fools and Horses*, but unlike the leader of the Trotter clan, Frankie's occasional dips into the French language were accurate.

Unwilling to dive in with both feet, Joe concentrated on her linguistic habit, and she was happy to explain. 'Back in the day, I lived in Belgium for a while, and I picked up the language.' She laughed throatily, and lit a cigarette. 'You do, don't you? Where was it your wife went to after you split up? Spain or somewhere? I bet she's fluent in the local language now.'

'Canary Islands,' Joe corrected her, 'and you're right. She speaks it like a local. So where in Belgium were you? Brussels?'

'Hell, no. I couldn't afford to live there. No, I lived to the far north, in a little place called Knokke-Heist. Beautiful little town. Fabulous beach.'

The slightest of doubts entered Joe's head, but he put them aside. 'I don't wanna take up too much of your time, Frankie, but the word is you did your share of door-knocking on Kimbolton

Terrace, trying to get the residents to sell up.'

Frankie's features became more serious. 'Not as much as you might think, Joe, but yeah, we've done a fair bit of canvassing in that area. I know we can be a pain in the *fesse*, but it's a legitimate business exercise. If we knock on, say, two hundred doors, we might pick up two props. The homeowners are happy when we sell, the buyers are happy, and we make a good commission on it.'

Joe's phone rang. He checked the menu window, read "Gemma" and cut it off. Concentrating on Frankie, he homed in on his main question. 'Ever have any dealings with old Trelfus?'

'Did we ever? Dear God, he was an awful man, and it got to the stage where when we were knocking Kimbolton, we'd go past his door. I've never met anyone so abusive, and it was all right for the likes of Tel Bailey and Ian Parsloe. They were big enough to deal with the silly old sod, but I couldn't do with his threatening. I wouldn't care, but it was the Social Services Department who put us onto him. According to them, he needed to come out of that house and go into care. They couldn't persuade him, but they told us that if we could get him out, the money he made on the sale would be enough to fund his care. In the end, we gave it up as a bad job. He was just a mean, cantankerous old *râleur*.'

'And you didn't see him at all the night you went to pick up Ros? The night Trelfus died?'

'No. And if I had, I'd have ignored him.'

Joe decided he could learn nothing more, and

stood up. 'Thanks for your time, Frankie. I don't think I'll need to bother you again.'

'No problem. Oh, how's – what's her name – Sheila Riley?'

'Sheila Naylor as she is these days. Still bad. Just goes to show you. She should have stuck to roast beef and Yorkshire pudding.'

Chapter Ten

The moment Joe climbed into his car, he took out his phone and returned Gemma's call.

'I was just letting you know that Martin is coming in at one o'clock. Don Oughton has authorised me to let you sit in the observation room while I conduct the interview with Vinny Gillespie. The Chief Super will be with you to make sure everything is above board.'

'What? They don't trust you?'

'Sanford's a small town, as you know, and everyone knows everyone. Sheila is an old friend, Joe, if only by proxy because you're my uncle. We have to be seen to do it right, and if anything comes of it, we'll have to call Roy Vickers from Wakefield or Ray Dockerty from Leeds.'

It made sense. 'I'll be there.' Joe checked his watch. 'I've time to nip back to The Lazy Luncheonette to make sure everything's in order for lunches, and then I'll be with you.'

His excitement rising at the prospect, he battled once again with the Sanford traffic, fighting his way back to the café, where he found everything in order and under Brenda's control.

'Have you learned anything?' she asked as the door opened and George Robson walked in.

'Yes. I've learned that even though Sanford is only a small place, it never ceases to surprise you. George Robson walking into my place is like the angel showing up to guide the three wise men to the manger.'

'It was a star, actually, Joe,' George said.

George was chargehand in the leisure services department, looking after Sanford's parks and gardens, and along with Brenda and Sheila, he was one of Joe's oldest friends. All the same, it was a surprise to see him. In common with most of the local authority's employees, he preferred the subsidised canteen at the town hall. A large man in all directions, vertical and horizontal, he was by any definition a heavy drinker, but he lived by a credo similar to Brenda's: enjoy life while you can because you're a long time dead. Along with his close friend, Owen Frickley, he attended all the 3rd Age Club events and joined them on all the outings, but on the excursions, they went their own way rather than taking part in any organised events.

A man like George, Joe decided, would have been ideal for dealing with Kimberry, Joe put the proposition to him, he cried off.

'I'd love to help, Joe. I know Bob Kimberry, and nothing would give me greater pleasure than to paste him all over Sanford, but there's a coupla problems with that. First off, he's twenty years younger than me, and I'd need Owen with me, and secondly I'm in the middle of a working day. That wouldn't normally a problem, but Kimberry's boss, Parsloe, has connections at the town hall. His sister's husband works in the Planning Department. Snooty git. He'd report me for skiving off.' George settled down with a portion of Joe's steak and kidney pudding and vegetables.

'Anyroad up, you've got Lee, and he can deal with Kimberry and Parsloe.'

Joe put a beaker of tea before his old friend, and joined him. 'Fair enough. So what brings you to The Lazy Luncheonette?'

'You keep bragging about your steak and kidney pud, so I thought I'd give it a try.' George munched on a mouthful of food and swallowed it, washing it down with a healthy swig of tea. 'Besides, I'd heard you were looking into Sheila's husband.'

Joe was uncharacteristically reluctant to talk. 'Where did you hear that?'

George laughed and chewed more food. 'Everybody in Churchill's heard the argument last night.' He cast a glance about the café, a look which took in Brenda. 'Are you two accusing him of trying to murder her?'

'It's a bit complicated, George. Do you know something?'

'No. What?'

Joe shook his head in his exasperation. 'I didn't mean I was going to tell you something. I'm asking whether you know anything at all.'

'Oh. Right. Not really, but it was something Sheila asked a few weeks ago. Mid-November-ish. She has a holly bush in the back garden, and she was worried that it wasn't producing berries. I told her that it needs to be in place for four or five years before they show, but she says it's been there since before Pete died, and she's sure she's had berries from it before.'

Joe's brow creased. 'I think she may be right.

I do remember her making a holly wreath one Christmas, and that had berries on it. I don't understand why this matters, George.'

'Those berries are poisonous, Joe.' George took a healthy swallow of tea, and attacked his meal again. 'I'm not saying you could top someone with them, but you'd certainly give them the trots and make them throw up.'

By now, the conversation had attracted Brenda's attention, and leaving the counter to one of Cheryl's friends, she joined them. 'Are you suggesting Martin could be feeding her the berries?'

George shrugged. 'Search me. I reckon she'd notice if he was. I'm just saying that she was complaining that this tree isn't flowering like it should, and now she's falling sick every five minutes.'

'And you're sure the tree's not dead?' Joe asked.

'Certain of it. In fact, I thought Sheila had it wrong. I'd swear it was no older than a coupla years. But then, what do I know? I'm only a thick gardener, aren't I?' George grumbled on as he ate. 'Only been at it since I left school. How would I know what I'm talking about?'

Joe and Brenda exchanged a look swamped with the kind of worries which had plagued them for the last two days. 'You didn't notice whether the soil had been disturbed?' Joe asked. 'As if it'd been replanted.'

George polished off the last of his meal, pushed the plate to one side and ran a paper serviette over his mouth before taking a large swallow of tea. 'Grand that, Joe. Just what I needed to line the stomach for a good session tonight. And no, I didn't notice. She rang me after work one night, and it was pitch bloody dark in the garden. I told her I'd need to see it in daylight if I was gonna give her a proper opinion. She told me not to bother, so I didn't. I don't mind doing favours for friends, but I do have a life to lead.'

Joe and Brenda exchanged glances again. 'We need to get a look at that tree,' Joe said.

'Fat chance,' Brenda retorted. 'After last night, if we rang the doorbell, she'd release the hounds.'

In the act of finishing his tea, George's eyes widened and he put the beaker down. 'Are you two for real? You really think Martin's trying to shuffle her off?'

'I told you, it's complicated.'

'Why would he?' George demanded.

'How about a quarter of a million quid?'

Brenda augmented Joe's question. 'That's how much Sheila is insured for.'

A look of thunder crossed George's chubby features. 'Leave him to me. I'll have him. Nobody threatens one of our gang.'

Joe checked his watch. 'Yeah, well, right now it's up to the Sanford police, and I'm due at Gale Street in half an hour. Thanks for the tipoff, George. I'll pass it on to Gemma. Give him a good discount on his dinner, Brenda.'

George screwed up his face again, in puzzlement this time. 'Discount? I thought it'd be free.'

'The tea was free.' Joe grinned savagely. 'They say miracles happen at Christmas, George, but you're forgetting that I don't do Christmas.'

'Scrooge.'

With the final complaint, George paid for his meal (discounted by twenty percent) and left them to it. As the first of the lunchtime customers began to form a queue, Joe moved behind the counter, Brenda marshalling the team in the kitchen, and they went into familiar action.

'You know what we need, don't you?' Joe said.

'A lottery win?'

With a scowl, he took the first order from the woman at the front of the queue, and passed it to the kitchen. While pouring out a cup of tea for the customer, he muttered to Brenda, 'We need to do what we did in Whitby.'

Brenda frowned. 'We were on a treasure hunt in Whitby, Joe.'

Joe rang up the sale, and gave the woman change. 'Yes, but between times, Maddy and I carried out a little burglary.'

The light dawned in Brenda's eyes. 'Yes, but Sheila's place is likely to be better alarmed than the shabby little place you broke into. And as I recall, you and Maddy got nicked that night.'

Joe rang up the second sale, and handed over change. 'It's in a good cause, Brenda. How about it? Nine, ten o'clock tonight?'

She resigned herself to the inevitable. 'Let's see how you get on at the police station first.'

* * *

Joe was at Gale Street a few minutes before Gemma was scheduled to begin questioning Martin, and both she and Chief Superintendent Don Oughton were at pains to warn him off.

'This is serious business, Joe,' Oughton said, 'and we can't have any interference. You're welcome to observe, you're welcome to pass any comments to me, and if I think they are valid, I'll put them through to Gemma via the headset. But you can't confront Martin. And I know you. Even if you face him later – and I know for a fact you will – you mustn't give any hint that you were here in the police station.'

Joe had known Don Oughton for almost as long as he had known Sheila and Brenda, and although he was never intimidated by the Chief Superintendent's rank, common sense prevailed. 'You have my word, Don.'

Oughton gave Gemma the nod, and she and Detective Constable Vinny Gillespie stepped into the interview room while Joe and the station commander entered the observation room.

Martin appeared quite calm while Gemma ran through the pre-interview process. He had a bottle of still water close to hand, and drank occasionally from it while she gave him the background information necessary to conduct the interrogation.

Sat in the cramped observation room, Joe could hear everything, and Gemma was wearing an earpiece through which Oughton could communicate with her.

'These matters have been brought to our attention, Mr Naylor, by North Shires Insurance. It's not up to me to question their methods, so I can't say how they came by the information, but given the documents they've supplied, I do need to question you. You're not under caution, you are not obliged to answer any of my questions, but I would advise you to do so. The more information we have, the better our chances of clearing the business up. You're entitled to have a legal representative, or any other witness with you, if you wish. Do you want anyone with you?'

Martin smiled confidently. 'No. According to my wife, the best witness I could have at my side is Joe Murray, but I'm already aware that he's the one who passed the North Shires documents to you. And before you say anything more, Inspector, I'm also aware that you have a personal interest in this business. Joe Murray's your uncle, isn't he?'

'Irrelevant,' Gemma said. 'Yes, Joe is my uncle, but although I've known her for a good number of years, I have no relationship with your wife or with North Shires Insurance. I am the senior detective in Sanford CID, and it's my place to initiate enquiries. If we feel that further investigation is necessary, it will be passed to a superior officer from either Wakefield or Leeds. Satisfied?'

'Not entirely, but let's get this thing out of the way. I know what you're asking about. Murray and his friend, Mrs Jump, came to me with it yesterday, and I tell you in advance, it is nonsense.'

Gemma was not fazed by his bald assertion. 'Let's see, shall we?' She laid the evidence on the table and turned it all to face him. 'A couple of tragic stories from some years ago, and a photograph of your wedding party which appeared in the Sanford Gazette. I have to say, Mr Naylor, that you bear a striking resemblance to Mervyn Nellis and Marlon Newman. Roughly the same height, you have the same physique, similar facial structure. Given the lack of any alternative evidence, I would say that you are both Mervyn Nellis and Marlon Newman, and it's our belief, that both men are one and the same, and he or they are wanted in connection with the disappearance of Mrs Francine Nellis, and the suspicious death of Deirdre Ullsworth.'

Martin laughed. 'Exactly as Murray put it yesterday, although he wasn't quite so eloquent. Yes, I do look like Nellis and Newman, but I'm not either of them. Until your uncle brought this to me yesterday, I'd never even heard of them. I have no connection with Darlington or Ripon, and I defy you to demonstrate otherwise.'

'I can't,' Gemma confessed. 'I but I can ask for your fingerprints and a DNA swab, which we'll deal with at the end of this interview.'

'No problem. As long as I have your assurance that they will be destroyed when they demonstrate my innocence.'

'They will.'

Joe knew that fingerprints and a DNA swab would prove nothing. Marlon Newman's prints had never been taken for the simple reason that

Deirdre's death was initially assumed to be natural causes, and by the time the police came to a different conclusion, he had disappeared and any evidence in the house would have been long covered up. In the case of Mervyn Nellis, Banks had told him that fingerprints and DNA had been destroyed on Nellis's insistence, once his wife's disappearance was assumed to be nothing more sinister than that.

Gemma was not to be deterred. 'We ran a cursory check on you, Mr Naylor, and we can't find any trace of you until a few years ago. Coincidentally, shortly after Deirdre Ullsworth's death.'

Martin shrugged confidently. 'I'm sorry, Inspector, but I can't account for your inefficiencies. But I did tell Murray and Jump yesterday that I can point them – and you – to my first wife's grave, in York, my hometown.'

Gemma slid a pen and a sheet of paper across the table to him. 'If you would be so kind. And rest assured, we will check up on it.'

Martin carried on speaking as he wrote out the directions. 'She's buried at Fulford Cemetery, which I think, is one of the largest in York, and you may have problems finding her grave. Regrettably, I haven't visited in years, and I'm not sure I could find it.' He pushed the paper and pen back to Gemma. 'She died quite some time ago, and I was understandably very distressed. I lived alone for a long time afterwards, right up to meeting Sheila, as a matter of fact.'

Gemma took the handwritten instructions and

slotted them into the folder. 'All right, Mr Naylor, let's talk about Mrs Riley... Pardon me, Mrs Naylor, and her current health issues. I did indicate that I've known this lady for many years, and she's always enjoyed excellent health. In the three months since you and she married, she's gone downhill.'

'From which you assumed that I'm poisoning her.' Martin chuckled. 'I'm not a doctor, Ms Craddock, so I couldn't possibly explain her illness as well as a medic might. Be that as it may, notwithstanding all the tests Doctor Khalil, her GP has ordered, they have failed to satisfactorily explain the problem. I met with Doctor Khalil a few days ago, and he's firmly convinced that the cause of her problems is psychosomatic. Something to do with her absolute devotion to her former husband, and not wanting to upset me. Furthermore, don't pretend that you don't know this. I'm well aware of your relationship with Sheila's nephew, Howard, and I am practically certain he must have told you of these conclusions.'

'He did, but considering the documents we received from North Shires, and the history of these two men, both of whom you deny any knowledge, I have no choice but to broach the matter.' Gemma leaned forward, asserting herself. 'My concern, Mr Naylor, is that Sheila may unwittingly be harbouring a murderer.'

Martin laughed aloud this time. 'When you can prove that, Ms Craddock, by all means come back to me. Now is there anything else or can I go?'

In the observation room, Joe had a thousand and one questions he would have asked, but Gemma remained under the constraints of PACE, the Police and Criminal Evidence act, and she brought the session to an end.

As they left the interview room, Martin cast a humorous glance at the two-way glass behind which Joe and Don Oughton were sat. 'My condolences, Joe. It must be terrible to realise you're wrong.'

Chapter Eleven

After Martin left, they moved to Oughton's first floor office, overlooking Gale Street and the rear entrance to Galleries shopping mall. There was a brief discussion between Joe, Gemma and Oughton, which took place over a cup of bland, police canteen tea.

The chief superintendent was not entirely despondent, but neither was he particularly upbeat. 'If we run a full check on Naylor, it'll take days, maybe even weeks. If he really is Nellis or Newman, he could have disappeared before we get the results.'

'In the meantime, Sheila's life could still be in danger.' Joe's glum face brightened suddenly. 'Oh, I knew I had something to tell you.' They fixed their attention on him, and he related the tale George Robson had told him over lunch.

Oughton was particularly interested. 'George knows his stuff. Crikey, he's been working in parks and gardens for the last forty odd years. Are holly berries really poisonous?'

'Saponin, sir,' Gemma said. 'Not likely to be fatal, but it certainly could upset your gastric system.'

'That's what George said,' Joe confirmed, 'and if you think about it, it's exactly what's been wrong with Sheila.'

'We're walking on a tightrope,' Oughton declared. 'If we go barging into Sheila's place, looking for evidence, and we find nothing, she'll tear us to pieces. She'll rip us to shreds even if we do find something. Have you any ideas, Joe?'

Although he did not feel any humour, Joe grinned. 'Yes, but you don't wanna know about it. I'm not sure it's legal.'

Both police officers laughed, Gemma gave him a mild warning to watch his step, and a few minutes later, the debate petered out, and Joe left the station, to fight his way back to The Lazy Luncheonette.

'At least I can enjoy a decent cuppa here,' he said to Brenda while he detailed the interview to her.

With the time coming up to 3 o'clock, and the day's trade beginning to fade, he and Lee climbed into his car for yet another battle across Sanford – with a pause to fill the tank this time – and Parsloe's yard.

'Whatever you do, don't get stupid, Lee. I need you there just to counter the threat of this Kimberry character. I'll deal with Parsloe, and you don't have to get physical unless Kimberry tries his luck.'

'Don't worry, Uncle Joe. If he starts, I'll slap him about a bit. When I'm done with him, this Kimberley won't know his backside from his shoulder blade.'

Joe tutted. 'You mean his backside from his elbow.'

'I knew it were one of them joints.'

They drove past a large, out-of-town supermarket, with Santa Claus standing at the entrance, ringing his bell and rattling his charity tin. The storefront was decorated with Christmas trees and flashing lights, and the scene generated an almost childlike enthusiasm in Lee.

'Hey, you are coming to ours on Christmas Day, aren't you?'

'I'll be there, yes. I don't know when or how long I'll be staying. Someone has to look out for Sheila, and it's probably down to me and Brenda because I don't trust Martin.'

Leigh's face fell. 'Danny'll be disappointed if you don't show up. He always looks forward to you coming on Christmas Day with your presents.'

'I told you, I'll be there. Oh, while I think on, you do remember I'm taking him to see Santa in Galleries tomorrow. I'll pick him up sometime in the morning. Okay?'

'Cheryl knows about it, and we told Danny earlier this week. He's dead chuffed. He always is when you take him to Santa's grotto.'

Joe greeted the news with mixed feelings. He recalled a time when he was in the queue with Danny, and Santa, apparently drunk, collapsed. It turned out he had been poisoned, and the memory prompted Joe's worries for Sheila yet again.

But if Sheila was a matter for serious concern, he was actively anticipating the confrontation with Parsloc and Kimberry. Like too many people in this small mining community, they had underestimated his resourcefulness, and it was always satisfying to give such individuals a metaphorical kick where it would hurt the most, and judging from Kimberry's earlier reaction to

Lee, his giant nephew was exactly the advantage he needed.

Events were ahead of them. When he pulled into the street, the first thing he noticed outside Parsloe's yard, was the dark green, rusting van belonging to Bailey and Dixon, and he could only imagine the scene in the little hut. Kimberry was a big, tough man, but Joe doubted that he was any match for Tel Bailey, and it was almost certain that Parsloe wasn't.

Nothing had changed in the yard. It was as unkempt and disorganised as the previous day, but when the noise of a scuffle reached them from the shed, he and Lee burst in to discover that things were worse than Joe had anticipated.

Parsloe was slumped in his chair, apparently out for the count. Bailey had Kimberry by the throat, and was physically trying to lift him from the ground.

'Don't, Tel. Let him go.'

Bailey turned furious features on Joe and his nephew. 'I'm gonna smite him. They wasted that miserable old twonk, and left me to carry the can. Well, they're gonna pay for it.'

Joe pleaded with him. 'Put him down, Tel. We need to speak to both of them, and if you do him and Parsloe any serious damage, you really will end up doing a long stretch. Please, let him go.'

'He's dead meat.'

Lee pushed past Joe, grabbed Bailey's outstretched arm, and applied all his might, gradually lowering both the hand and Kimberry to the floor.

Bailey glowered at Lee, who glared back. 'Let him go, Tel, or you'll reckon with me.'

Bailey's eyes sent burning spears of lightning by return. 'You're next, Murray.'

'It'll take someone bigger than you, Bailey. Now get your maulers off him.'

Part of Joe's mind detached from the urgency of the situation, and pondered the potential maelstrom of a straight fight between Bailey and Lee. The outcome was uncertain. Bailey kept himself in peak condition, but Lee had lost none of his strength or aggression since giving up his rugby career, and he, too, kept himself fit with regular sessions in the gym. It was almost certain that the shed would be wrecked, but who would be the victor? Joe did not know, but as a matter of self-preservation he was prepared to run for it before the real scrap started.

Kimberry's features were turning bright red. Lee clasped Bailey's large hands in a desperate effort to pry them away from his throat. Joe, helpless in most situations like this, decided to lend a hand. He was wearing only a pair of trainers, but he nevertheless kicked Bailey on the shin.

'Ouch.'

The exclamation came from Joe, but the blow must have got through. Bailey released Kimberry who staggered to the back of the hut, and flopped into a vacant chair, gasping for breath, while Tel rubbed his shin and turned a furious face on Joe.

Unable to dominate the situation physically, Joe had no qualms in facing down the angry builder. 'Have you completely lost the plot? Or have you been filling up at the Boat & Horses again?'

'I haven't been nowhere near the Boat & Horses or any other pub. And it was them what killed the bloke. I guarantee it. They tried to have me walled up for it.'

'Right and that's what we're here to find out, Tel, and by your own admission, you can't remember what you were doing through that night. Now calm down and let me deal with the questions.'

Parsloe began to recover. He had a prominent black eye, presumably where Bailey's knuckles had connected with it, and as he came to and took in the opposition, he staggered from his seat, and moved to the rear of the hut alongside his minder, his eyes wide with terror and the prospect of the two oversized men facing him. 'You… you just get out of here, Bailey, and you Murray. Or I'll call the cops.'

Bailey, unimpressed with the bluster, was about to go on the offensive again, but Joe stopped him, and stepped forward. 'Blow it out the window, Parsloe. You want the police here, send for them, and while they're here I'll be talking to them about the threatening behaviour of your beefcake when he called at The Lazy Luncheonette this morning.' He waved an erratic hand at the direction of Kimberry, still cowering alongside his employer, whooping in large gulps of air. 'You have questions to answer about the old boy at fifteen Kimbolton Terrace, and if you don't answer them then *I'll* call the cops.'

'Old Billy Trelfus was nothing to do with us.'

'You know his name, though.'

'Everyone knows him. Everyone except this moron and his mate Dixon.'

Parsloe waved a hand at Tel as the "moron" in question, and Bailey took a threatening step forward, only to be held back by Lee.

'Nark it, Tel,' Lee ordered.

'He just called me a moron.'

'So tell him you're really a Catholic.'

Joe groaned at his nephew's response. 'Moron not Mormon, you idiot. Sometimes, Lee, I think you're just yanking our chain.'

Lee smiled mock-modestly. 'If I did that, Uncle Joe, it'd come away from your neck.'

Joe shook his head in bewilderment. 'I didn't mean it literally. Yanking your chain is a metaphor for fooling around.'

Now Lee blushed. 'You mean like when me and our Cheryl—'

Joe cut him off. 'Don't say it, Lee. I have enough on my plate without having to suffer mental images of you and your wife doing what comes naturally.' The other three had been looking on with mixed feelings of amazement and puzzlement. Joe rounded on Parsloe and Kimberry, and they honed their attention on his fiery features. 'Right, you two. You say everybody knew Billy Trelfus. I know loads of people in this town, but I didn't know him. So tell me about him.'

'We've been door-knocking in that area for the last two years.' Parsloe waved an erratic hand at Bailey. 'Him and Dixon have only been doing it for the six months, and they never went on the knock in Kimbolton above once or twice. They bought number seventeen at one of Hepple's auctions, so they didn't know him, but anybody who knocked on old Billy's door, salesmen, Bible bashers, even Help the rotten Aged and Social Services, always got a mouthful. He was a whingeing, whining, moaning old sod, and he'd lost half his marbles. When he opened the door, he'd always accuse you of doing something wrong. He accused me and Bob throwing stones at his window like some bloody schoolkids, and when it turned out, it was bloody schoolkids. He accused us of knocking holes in the plaster and we'd never even been in the place. Then he accused us of making it fall off by hammering on the walls next door and we'd never even been in there except to check it over before the auction. Seventeen was empty until Bailey and Dixon bought it, and we'd never worked for that blonde tart at number thirteen.'

'Eleven,' Joe corrected him in an effort to stem the overflow of information. 'There is no number thirteen.'

'Smartarse,' Parsloe sneered. 'Notice everything, don't you?'

'A damn sight more than you do.' Joe pointed an accusing finger at Kimberry. 'I notice he's about as subtle as a twenty ton truck, coming into my café and threatening me like that. Anyone prepared to do that wouldn't think twice about knocking an old boy on the head.'

'It wasn't us,' Parsloe insisted. 'He was just a narky and nasty piece of work, and I reckon his neighbours'll be cheering now he's snuffed it. And if you don't believe me, ask Frankie Hepple. She got enough mouth off him.'

'I already did ask her,' Joe retorted, and persisted with his determination to get to the truth. 'So where were you two on the night he was killed?'

'Home,' Parsloe replied. 'And the missus will verify that.'

'The same goes for me,' Kimberry declared.

Lee's eyes widened. 'What? His missus'll verify that you were with her? What kind of marriage have you got, Parsley?'

Joe shook his head again. 'Just ignore him. He'll come back to earth eventually.' He turned on the fire again and aimed it at the two, still shaking builders. 'And that's all you can tell us?'

'What more do you expect? We were nowhere near Kimbolton that night. End of story.' Parsloe once again flapped his hand in the direction of Bailey. 'He's the one who was dossing next door. He's more likely to have done it than us. Yes, and there's fat boy's missus. She had some ruck with him. Have you quizzed her?'

Bailey took a step forward, but Lee restrained him. Tel contented himself with raising the threat in his voice. 'Our Van?'

It was a comment from Lee that once again took the heat out of the moment. 'You mean that old rust bucket outside, Tel? I don't see how it could have an argument with this Tellpuss sort?'

John sighed. 'He means his sister. Vanessa. She's married to Denny Dixon.'

Lee laughed. 'You call your sister, Van? I bet that's awkward when you're talking about the price of petrol.'

This time, Joe groaned. 'Just forget it, Lee.' He rounded on Parsloe again. 'You've witnessed an argument between Vanessa Dixon and old Billy?'

With a wary eye on Bailey, Parsloe nodded. 'The day they bought number seventeen. She came to look at it, and he happened to be on his way back from the pub, or something. She ended up in a slanging match with him. And that's it, Murray. That's all we know.'

Kimberry nodded urgently, a silent agreement with his boss, and Joe decided to call it a day. 'There's nothing more you're gonna tell me, obviously. Just one last thing. Your moron came to my place this morning and offered me seventy-five for number seventeen Kimbolton. I'll tell you what I told him. You want it, it's yours, but I want a hundred and fifty for it as is.'

Parsloe felt bold enough to sneer once again. 'You know what you can do with it.'

Joe pointed a final, warning finger at him. 'In that case, keep Bob the Building away from my café, or next time I'll have Lee the Leg-breaker tie him in knots before I kick him out.' Joe turned on his heels and stormed from the hut, followed by Lee and Bailey and once outside in the icy, December drizzle, he gave Bailey a final warning. 'Keep out of it, Tel. I'm doing my best for you, but it's a waste of time if you go round threatening guys like that.'

'He was lying, Joe. All right, so I've never known him and Kimberry go that far before, but I do know they've threatened homeowners in the past. I reckon they topped Trelfus.'

'And that's gonna be difficult to prove, lad. What do you know about this argument between your Van and Billy Trelfus?'

'Nothing. At least, she's never said anything to me. You could ask Denny. But I'll tell you what, if Trelfus started with her, she would have given him a good mouthful back.'

'I'll speak to Denny and Van. Now get yourself back to Tandy Street.'

Bailey slid open the door of his van and prepared to climb in. 'Oh, Joe, by the way, talking of Tandy Street, there's no way that place is worth a hundred and fifty big ones. Done up, it might be worth one-twenty, but even then you'd be struggling.'

Joe jerked a thumb over his shoulder at his nephew, and said to Bailey, 'Now you're getting as daft as him.'

With the darkness of an early winter's night settling, Joe drove back to The Lazy Luncheonette, where Brenda let them in, and while Lee got into his own car to go home, Joe and Brenda locked the front door, and settled down with a cup of tea. Joe gave her a full account of the visit to Parsloe's, followed by a more detailed version of what had happened at the police station.

'We have to check out that holly bush,' he

concluded. 'George isn't often wrong about these things, and as matters stand, the police won't do anything without some form of evidence. Unless you've got any other ideas, I can't think where else to look. Are you up for it tonight?'

'It'll have to be late, Joe. Sheila isn't sleeping well, remember, and I dread the thought of how she'll react if she catches us.'

'Eleven o'clock tonight?' He could see the doubt in her face. 'Too early? All right then, how about midnight?'

She nodded. 'Pick me up… And hey, don't forget to bring a torch and a decent camera.'

Chapter Twelve

What is wrong with you? Are you so niggardly that you cannot even grant our mother some contentment?

We may live four thousand miles from the shoddy little town in Yorkshire where we were born, but we keep in constant contact with mother, and she's told us of your absurd and groundless allegations against Martin. It's a far cry from the man who wished her every happiness on her wedding day just three months ago.

Martin Naylor has brought our mother nothing but peace and the contentment she deserves after being on her own for so long, and his efforts to get the bottom of this inexplicable illness have been unstinting. What he and mother need is someone to bring pressure to bear on the medical services, and not a mean-spirited man and loose-legged woman consumed with envy.

Martin and our mother may be reluctant to press this business further, but unless you grow up and leave them alone, we will be in touch with the police with a view to prosecuting both of you.

Peter Jnr and Aaron Riley.

On reading the unexpected email, Joe's temper flashed. His hand shook as he prepared to type out an angry response, but in the time it took him to roll a cigarette and make a cup of tea, he'd calmed down sufficiently to ring Brenda, and after the initial exchanges, he read the email to her.

'Don't respond, Joe. You'll only make matters worse.'

His anger was on the rise again. 'Have you listened to one word I said? The names they call me... well, fair enough, I can take it, but they're slagging you off, too. I'm not going to sit by and let them—'

'They're Sheila's sons,' Brenda interrupted. 'If it was Sheila suspected of murder, they'd still defend her. That's what sons are for. According to their limited view of the situation, Martin makes Sheila happy, and that's all that matters.'

'And when she turns up dead in a month, who will they blame? You and me for not doing anything to stop it.'

Brenda breathed out heavily. 'Boys are always closer to the mother, Joe, and it doesn't matter what the reality of the situation is... At least until they have to confront it. We are wrong, even if we're right, because Sheila tells them we're wrong. Just ignore it. Are we still on for raiding their back garden tonight?'

'After getting this kind of abuse from her boys? Just try and keep me away.'

'Then pick me up about midnight as we arranged.'

After microwaving a quick meal, Joe spent most of the evening running through his notes on the killing of Billy Trelfus. There were outstanding questions he would have to confront, not least of which was a few words with Vanessa Dixon. He knew her of course. Most of Sanford did, and she was more like her brother than her husband; aggressive. Nevertheless, sometime over the weekend, he would have to find the time to speak to her.

The lack of firm evidence on any front was a big stumbling block. Suspicion fell on Tel purely and simply because he was next door, unable to recall anything of the previous night (which in Joe's opinion declared him innocent). It was much more likely that someone else had called after Tel had slipped into drunken oblivion. But who? Frankie and Ros Hepple were both there at different times. Was it possible that one of them had done the deed? Frankie (according to the woman herself and Ian Parsloe) had suffered some of Trelfus's vitriol in the past.

It was a personal judgement, but Joe could not see either of them resorting to violence. Not unless they were provoked.

When it came to the matter of Martin Naylor, he had not shifted his belief that the man was also Mervyn Nellis and Marlon Newman, and despite the refusal of Sheila and her two sons to confront the issue, he represented a serious threat to her life. For Joe's money, Martin had been far too cocky and confident in the police station. Anyone pulled in, facing the possibility of such serious charges, should have been jittery to say the least. Martin was anything but. Right down to a level of sarcasm which rivalled Joe's, he had been too comfortable in his denials. Martin Naylor, however, did not know Joe Murray. In fact, it was practically certain that he had never met anyone with Joe's doggedness.

At just after eleven o'clock, he changed from his jeans and shirt, into a pair of black jogging pants and a black sweater, an outfit he had often used for fancy dress parties when he went as Darth Vader. His trainers, unfortunately, were mostly white with flashes of blue, so he left those behind, and put on a pair of solid, black shoes. Noise, he reasoned, would not be a problem in Sheila's back garden. He completed the ensemble with a black woolly hat, and at eleven thirty, climbed into his car for the short journey to Brenda's place.

She too had dressed in similar jogging pants and jumper, with a pair of black running shoes, but refused to wear anything on her head. 'I've just had my hair done for Christmas and I don't want to crash in for an emergency appointment at the hairdressers on Tuesday morning.'

'I wouldn't give you a Tuesday morning off anyway.'

'I know, but then, I wouldn't ask your permission.'

The weather outside was still bitterly cold, but the rain had stopped, and clear skies settled over Sanford. Winter stars gleamed in the night, and the air temperature plummeted. They were fine in Joe's car, which although it had many years under its fan belt, was nevertheless possessed of an excellent heater, but once they parked around the corner from Larch Avenue where Sheila could not possibly see the vehicle, they felt the cold snapping at them as they made their way surreptitiously down the back lane between the streets.

They had driven along past the front of the bungalow and confirmed that the house was in darkness, and as they trod the back lane, Joe kept his voice down and asked, 'Does she have security lights covering the back garden?'

'Not that I know of. The house is locked up like Fort Knox, and everyone knows she's the widow of a police inspector. Her house has been a no-go area for every burglar in town since forever. Plus, she gets all sorts of wildlife in the garden. Hedgehogs and stuff. Even a fox and a couple of badgers once over. They'd trigger a PIR, wouldn't they?'

'Ask me about steak and kidney pies and puddings, and I can answer you. Hedgehogs, foxes and badgers are beyond my brief.'

They reached the rear gate of Sheila's bungalow, and Joe tried the latch only to find it locked.

'Bolted on the inside,' Brenda whispered. She bent slightly at the knee and cupped her hands.

'Shouldn't I be lifting you up?' Joe asked.

'You're lighter than me.'

'Remember you're the one who said that.'

He placed one foot in her hands and pushed himself upwards. Brenda lifted at the same time, and almost immediately released his foot, unable to hold his weight. Joe was able to grab the top of the tall gate and haul himself up.

Clinging on grimly, he whispered, 'There's a faint light coming from the bathroom.'

'It's from the hall,' Brenda responded.

'Martin's insisted on leaving it on while Sheila's ill. Just in case she has to go to the bathroom during the night. He doesn't want her wandering around in total darkness.'

Joe reached over the gate and scrabbled for the bolt, but when he found it, it would not move. He realised that it was his weight pressing the bolt tight against its staple. He applied one foot to the gatepost, pushed back and as the gate wobbled, he slid back the bolt. At the same time, Brenda tried the latch, with unfortunate effects. Now unbolted, the gate swung open, carrying Joe with it. Unable to stop it all he could do was hang on, and he realised with total horror, that the freewheeling gate would crack into a tall, rough concrete post, from which one end of Sheila's washing line was suspended.

Aside from probably knocking him off the gate, the collision would be nothing, but he was concerned with the amount of noise it might make, and with no idea how light Sheila and Martin might sleep, he could not allow it.

Clinging on for dear life, he put out his arm, hand crooked at the wrist, palm facing outwards to prevent the collision. He was surprised how much it stung, but it nevertheless stopped the gate's inexorable journey. It wobbled uneasily on its hinges, and Joe, breathing a silent sigh of relief, dropped quietly to the ground.

He glared Brenda. 'Thank you for nothing. I almost broke my bloody wrist on that post.'

Her voice was a sniping whisper. 'I didn't know the flaming thing was going to swing open, did I?'

'Let's just get on with it, shall we? Where is this holly bush?'

Brenda waved through the open gate, vaguely to one side of the house. 'If I remember right, it's somewhere over in the corner. You can see it through the patio doors in the dining room.'

Joe looked around the garden and could see very little. There was no moon to guide them, only starlight, augmented by the thin light coming through frosted glass of the bathroom window.

'Stick to the hedges,' he whispered. 'That way, if anyone does come to the door, we're less likely to be seen.'

He crept into the garden, skirted round the open gate, and once past the offending washing post, pressed himself back to the hedgerows and began to sidle his way along. Brenda was close to him, her breath coming in short, nervous gasps.

'Scared or just excited at being this close to me?'

'Full of it tonight, aren't you?' she whispered.

Joe reached the corner of the garden, where the banks of hedgerow turned through ninety degrees. They were hidden from the house by the barren branches of a small apple tree. Joe recalled Sheila complaining that in all the years the tree had been there, she had never seen anything more than the occasional seed apple.

Peering through the sparse branches, he checked the house for signs of life, saw nothing, and risked shining his light along the hedgerows in search of the holly bush.

'You're sure George has this right? She does have a holly bush?'

'Definitely. One of her favourites. Especially at this time of year. It's further down there.' Brenda waved a hand through the darkness and towards the house.

He sucked in his breath. 'Okey-dokey.'

He began to creep along the hedgerows again. Underfoot, the grass was becoming slippery. Moisture in the air freezing as the temperature dropped, and coating the lawn with a thin sheen of ice. That was his diagnosis. But it made him more cautious. Progress was slow as he ensured that he put his foot down firmly after every step.

And as they edged forward, he could not help thinking about his flat. What was he doing playing pretend burglar on a perishing cold night like this? He could have been at home, tucked up in his warm bed, or sitting by the radiator in the living room, enjoying a warming glass of whisky, or perhaps a hot mug of tea, channel-hopping in the faint hope of finding something worthwhile to watch on television. He could be soaking in a hot bath. Anything would be preferable to sneaking around and shivering in Sheila's back garden.

He could imagine her and Martin snuggled up together in bed. Not doing anything, just huddling close together, and it brought to mind his exertions in Brenda's bedroom the previous night. Even without the inevitable intimacy (inevitable because he and Brenda went back a long way and it was her wont) he would prefer to be cuddled up close to her than watching his step on this freezing grass.

His thoughts must have distracted his concentration for a moment. His foot slipped from under him, and he went down, twisting the other ankle.

'Sh—'

'Shh.' Brenda cut off the curse before it could materialise . 'You'll wake them up.'

'I've broken me bloody ankle.'

'And if you don't shut up, I'll kick the other one and break that. Then you won't know which leg to limp on, will you?'

The ice and damp were already beginning to soak through Joe's jogging pants. He rubbed irritably at his injured ankle, and with Brenda's help he got to his feet.

'You can stand on it,' she declared. 'It's not broken.'

'You're a doctor as well? Maybe we should have got you to analyse Sheila's problems.'

'Just shut it and get a move on. At this rate, we'll be here all night, and you have to open The Lazy Luncheonette at six.'

But they did not need to go any further. When Joe flashed his light along the hedgerows, the elusive holly bush was there, right in front of them.

He understood now why it had been so difficult to see. It was buried in amongst the evergreen hedges, fighting for its rightful place with them. During daylight, the different shape and shade of its foliage – spikier and a lighter green than the hedgerow – would have been easy to spot, but with only a dim flashlight to guide them and a view along the line of bushes rather than face on, it was nigh-on impossible.

Joe got down on his knee again and shone his light under the bush. Sure enough, there were signs that the soil had been disturbed, which to him signalled that it had been planted only recently. George had got it right.

He stood and handed Brenda his compact camera. 'The flash is set. I'll prise the branches apart and shine my light on it. All you have to do is take the picture when you can see the soil underneath. Okay?'

'Gotcha.'

He crouched down again, and began to pull the branches open. It was harder work than he anticipated. Young the tree might be, but those slim twigs and branches were stout, determined to stay in place. Eventually, he managed to open up a gap wide enough for Brenda to aim the camera. She leaned forward, checked the image on the compact's tiny screen and pressed the shutter.

At that same instant, the garden was flooded with bright light from a security lamp above the double patio doors, now open with Martin and Sheila framed in them. Joe was so surprised that he let go of the branch he was holding back, and it whipped forward, whacking Brenda in the eye. She recoiled with language Joe could not be sure he had ever heard her use. The draymen, yes, but never Brenda.

On the patio doors, Martin was laughing. Sheila, wrapped in a housecoat was exactly the opposite. Arms folded, she glared daggers at both of them. 'If you want to take pictures of our garden, Murray, why don't you just say so? You could have come during the day.'

Joe's temper was beginning to get the better of him again. While Brenda rubbed at her eye, he turned, took a pace towards the couple, and his ankle reminded him of its tenderness.

'How long have you been watching us?'

'Ever since I heard you climbing on the gate.' Martin tapped his ears one at a time. 'I have twenty-twenty hearing, and I heard you sliding the bolt back.'

Joe waved an erratic hand Brenda, now taking a tissue to her eye. 'We have proof. This bushes has been recently replanted and—'

Martin cut him off. 'Yes, it has.'

Joe leapt on the admission. 'You see. He's trying to poison you, Sheila.'

Her reply was not much more than a hiss. 'Oh, for heaven's sake grow up, will you? Of course he replanted it.'

Joe was gobsmacked. Brenda stopped and stared with one good eye.

'You mean you knew?'

'Naturally. Martin told me all about it.'

Her husband grinned. 'I'm not the world's best gardener, and I damaged the original bush rather badly when I was mowing the lawn. The least I could do was dig it out, and replace it.'

Joe was still struggling for words. 'But George Robson…'

'Martin told me what had happened after I spoke with George,' Sheila said. 'And now, both of you, get off my property before I call the police.'

Joe was not surprised by the threat, but Brenda felt it necessary to plead their case. 'Sheila. Please. Everything we've done is with the absolute best of intentions. We're sorry.'

'So am I,' Sheila said. 'I never want to see or speak to either of you again.'

She turned and marched into the house. Brenda took one pace towards the patio doors, but Joe stayed her.

His face still split in a broad grin, Martin said, 'You can leave the way you came. Don't bother climbing over the gate to bolt it shut, Murray. I'll do that when you've gone.'

Chapter Thirteen

Joe noticed that when Brenda woke on Saturday morning, the first thing she did was examine her eye where the flailing branch had struck her. It was red and slightly swollen, but there would be no permanent damage. After using an eyebath, it was simple enough to cover with a little, carefully applied eye-shadow.

'Two nights this week we've spent together,' Joe said when she returned to the bedroom where he was dressed. 'We need to watch it before it becomes a habit.'

'I didn't notice you complaining last night.'

Joe responded with a grunt. 'I don't have time for an argument. I'll get off down to The Lazy Luncheonette and open up. You know I'm taking young Danny to see Santa once the breakfast rush is over?'

At the mention of the child's name, Brenda's surly mood lifted. 'He's a lovely little lad, and he so looks forward to you taking him to the Christmas grotto every year.' Her mouth turned sour again. 'God knows why, but he must be the only male in town who's happy to see you.'

Joe slid his feet into his shoes. 'What about the draymen? It doesn't matter how much I insult them, they still turn up and hand over their money.' He made for the door. 'I'll see you down there when you're ready.'

The engine of his car chugged reluctantly into

life a few minutes later, and he drove gingerly out of the street, testing the steering for the danger of black ice on the untreated side roads. Soon he was on Leeds Road, making his way more confidently to his home, where he changed into his working clothes, and then made his second journey of the morning to Britannia Parade. But while he scooted along on automatic pilot, he was mentally running through the previous night's disaster. He had no idea whether Sheila would go ahead with the threat to inform the police. As far as he was concerned, he and Brenda had suffered enough. As if to complement her damaged eye, his forearms were covered in scratches, and his ankle still hurt when he slipped and twisted it.

Worst was Martin's lame excuse and Sheila's casual acceptance of it as a measure of his love for her, his simple desire to make life as pleasant as possible, and his utter determination not to upset her. Not for the first time, he had to ask himself how Sheila had managed to become so gullible in so short a time. And not only Sheila. Her sons, too. Pulling around the rear of the café, killing the engine and digging into his pockets for the keys to the café, he shuddered at the memory of the angry email from Peter Jnr and Aaron. He would have replied had not Brenda advised against it. As he opened the rear door and killed the intruder alarm, Lee's Ford Focus come along the back lane, and spun into place alongside Joe's beat up old Vauxhall.

'Morning, Uncle Joe,' Lee greeted him with his customary air of indefatigable good cheer.

'A good job you didn't say good morning.'

Joe lit a cigarette and stood in the open rear doorway. As he pushed past, Lee noticed his uncle's limp. 'Have you hurt yourself?'

'No. I'm rehearsing for a part as Captain Hook in Peter Pan.'

As usual, Lee was unable to differentiate between the truth and raw sarcasm. 'Oh. Right. You're taking up amateur melodrama. That's what Martin teaches. Him as what married Auntie Sheila. Him as is trying to kill her.'

Joe thought about putting him right, but so early in the day, he couldn't be bothered with the argument. 'Get the hobs on, get breakfast under way. I'll just finish my smoke and open up for the mob.'

'Aye, aye, Cap'n.' Lee grinned. 'D'yer gerrit, Uncle Joe? You're gonna be Captain Buck and I said—'

'Yeah, yeah. Very droll.' A couple of minutes later, having satisfied his craving for nicotine, Joe flicked the half-smoked cigarette out into the night, and closed the back door. 'Now, let's get on with the breakfast.'

By the time Brenda arrived at seven o'clock, they had already served half a dozen truckers, most of them in a hurry to be back on the road, presumably making their way home to some distant location, and as the draymen began to turn up, it was, as usual, all hands to the pumps, a tougher proposition this morning as they were without Cheryl, who was at home, child minding, catering for an overexcited son who, according to

Lee, was hyperactively waiting for his Uncle Joe and the promised visit to Santa.

The cynical and good-natured banter between Joe and the draymen was the stuff of legends. It had been a feature of the breakfast period at The Lazy Luncheonette ever since Joe took over the running of the establishment from his father, a quarter of a century previously, and Joe was more than equal to every barbed witticism from the other side of the counter.

It did not take the draymen long to latch on to Joe's limp, causing one of the drivers, a regular named Len, to comment, 'You've been trying it on with Brenda, haven't you, and she's given you a good kick to keep you in your place.'

Joe was in the act of pulling out of beaker of tea, and thinking up a snappy rejoinder, when Lee leaned through the kitchen hatch, and said, 'You won't be saying that when he's famous for playing Captain Muck.'

Joe shook his head sadly, fervently wishing he had ignored Lee earlier on. 'He means Captain Hook.'

Len frowned. 'You're gonna be playing Captain Hook?'

Joe jerked a thumb over his shoulder. 'He thinks I am. I think I'm gonna carry on standing here and taking a fortune off you guys.'

'And while everyone else is rocking around the Christmas tree,' Brenda commented, 'Joe will be limping round it.'

Len also noticed her heavily made-up eye, but he was more cautious when dealing with Brenda.

'Accident?' he asked.

She shook her head and grinned. 'Joe thumped me. My fault. I spilled half a cup of tea.'

The man in question cut in on the banter. 'When we've all done taking the p... mickey, can we get on? I have to see Santa later this morning.' Which comment only gave rise to another round of ribaldry from both drivers and staff.

Cheryl's two friends, Pauline and Kayleigh arrived at half past eight and helped ease some of the pressure, but even with the departure of the draymen, as busy over the weekend as they were Monday through Friday, the queue never really eased off. Shoppers, many of them haggard-faced men with their wives and children in tow, chose The Lazy Luncheonette as better value than the fast food outlets in the nearby retail park, and it was fully eleven o'clock before Joe could settle at table five for a bite to eat and a quick cup of tea.

'I don't have long,' he said to Brenda. 'Danny'll be waiting for me.'

'No worries, Joe. I'm sure we'll cope. You won't be gone long, will you?'

'With the Galleries' track record on the queues around Santa's grotto, I should be back before tomorrow morning.'

He was about to down the last of his tea when his niece walked in, her face set in a mask of disapproval.

'You're in trouble, Joe,' she announced.

'I'm pleased to see you, too.'

'Good morning, Gemma,' Brenda said with more than hint of worry in her eyes.

Gemma ignored Joe's sarcastic reply, and responded to Brenda. 'You too. Martin Naylor has registered a complaint against you both.'

Joe groaned and rubbed his ankle, Brenda flopped down in the chair next to him, and Gemma sat opposite.

'Bring Inspector Craddock a cup of tea, Kayleigh,' Joe called over his shoulder, and then concentrated on his niece. 'So, are you charging us or just giving us the verbal?'

'The latter.' Gemma accepted a beaker of tea from Kayleigh. 'The Chief Super refuses to let me book you, but it is trespass and it's illegal. There's a danger that Naylor will go for the throat if you don't stop accusing him of trying to murder Sheila.'

'Tell me something,' Joe insisted. 'How will you all feel when he does a bunk and we find Sheila's body?' Gemma was about to read the riot act once again, but Joe held up his hands for silence. 'Yeah, yeah, I know what you're gonna say. But the medics are taking no notice of her tummy troubles, and you're not taking our concerns seriously.'

'Bring me one scrap of evidence and I will go to town on it. But what do you have? A resemblance to a known killer, Sheila suffering with an unidentified gastric problem, and the word of a bloody idiot like George Robson, and although George was right, it's been explained to you. Until something serious happens, do us all a favour. Back off.'

In acquiescing, Brenda sought to exculpate

herself and Joe. 'Like I said to Sheila last night, we did it with the best of intentions.'

'The road to Hell,' Gemma retorted.

'And we were the ones who came away injured,' Joe protested.

'Serves you right. If you want to spend Christmas in the nick, carry on as you are. On the other hand, if you want to poke your nose into things, sort out Tel Bailey and Billy Trelfus.'

'I tried,' Joe confessed. 'And I didn't get very far with that.'

'Yes, well, we've had his granddaughter in screaming at us. Not that we can tell her much. I'll send her to you. Maybe she can give you something to get your teeth into.'

Joe checked his watch. 'She'll have to wait. I'm due to take Danny to see Santa. I'll catch you all later.'

'Just think on,' Gemma warned. 'Any more of this, and I'll go over Oughton's head and book the pair of you.'

Joe removed his whites, put on his topcoat before stepping out through the rear door and climbing into his car.

Lee lived close to Joe, in a neat little townhouse which he and Cheryl had bought when they first married. That was in the days when he had a promising career in rugby, before the knee injury ended it. He never spoke about his financial situation, but Joe paid him as much as he could. Cheryl was more forthcoming, and frequently told Joe that money was often a problem, especially with Danny growing up.

As he collected her and her excited son, and began the drive into Sanford and Santa's grotto in the Galleries mall, Cheryl admitted that since Lee had become a junior partner in The Lazy Luncheonette, the financial pressure had eased a little.

'We're not absolutely flush, Joe, but that profit share doesn't half come in handy.'

Joe was relieved to hear it. One of his biggest fears had always been that Lee would be tempted by the lure of a large, top-class restaurant. By making him (and Brenda, and Sheila) partners in the business, he had averted the threat.

But if the move solved one problem, the latest turn of events had created another. Sheila was a partner in the business, but her attitude of previous night indicated that she wanted nothing to do with either him or Brenda again. That opened up the possibility of her demanding her share of the business in cash. They had never paid for their share. It was a gift from Joe, but when the articles were laid out by his lawyers, it granted then a percentage of the value of the business. If he and Brenda were right, and Martin Naylor really was Mervyn Nellis and Marlon Newman, he would encourage Sheila to demand her share. Even if it turned out that Martin was innocent, it may still be a hurdle Joe would have to get over, and although he did not know how much the final bill would be, he knew it would be expensive.

When they reached Galleries, the queue for Santa's Grotto was at least twice the length of the queue formed by the Sanford Brewery draymen every morning, and while Joe waited with Danny, Cheryl disappeared to catch up with some shopping.

'I hope Santa's not drunk this year, Uncle Joe,' Danny commented as they shuffled forward with the queue.

The child's simple comment, spoke volumes to Joe. Although it was a couple of years in the past, Danny obviously recalled the time when Santa had been "drunk". In fact, Santa had been poisoned, but Danny's parents (with Joe's agreement) felt that the boy was not ready to take in the awful impact of the truth.

A half hour after joining the people, they emerged from the other side, Danny having assured Santa that he had been on his absolute best behaviour all year, for which he received a toy car, the likes of which Joe could have bought him for a couple of pounds in many of the surrounding shops, they linked up with Cheryl in Ma's Pantry, where she had already secured coffee and cakes for herself and Joe, a soft drink and ice cream for Danny.

'Some woman's been looking for you, Joe,' Cheryl said as he stirred brown sugar into his coffee.

Joe chuckled. 'I should be so lucky.'

'No, seriously. I was in Collins's picking up a new tie for Lee, and I got talking to Mary Henley. You know her. Big friend of my mum's. She was saying as how there's this blonde thirty-something going round all the shops, asking for you.' Cheryl grinned. 'Hey, you haven't got a bit on the side, have you?'

'I repeat. I should be so lucky. Why would anyone – especially a young blonde – be looking for me?'

Cheryl laughed again. 'Maybe she's heard about the biscuit tin under your floorboards, where you keep your money.'

Danny's eyes popped. 'You keep your money in a biscuit tin, Uncle Joe? My dad keeps his in his wallet.'

'Yes, Danny, but if your mum's buying him ties from Collins' he won't have as much as me to put in a biscuit tin.' He focused on Cheryl again. 'I don't know who this woman is, and I don't know why she should be looking for me here, but if she's been asking around, someone must have pointed her to The Lazy Luncheonette.'

When he returned to his café, after dropping Cheryl and Danny back home, there was news waiting for him, but it had nothing to do with a thirty-something blonde.

'Les Tanner's had a complaint from Sheila, and called a special meeting,' Brenda told him. 'Half past twelve tomorrow lunchtime. Les wouldn't speculate on the agenda, but you're on it.'

Joe might have expected it. As club secretary, Sheila had been instrumental in drawing up the articles, and he was sure that there were clauses relevant to personal disputes between members, especially disputes where the behaviour of one member towards another could be called into question.

Joe sighed. 'Strange, blonde women chasing me in Galleries, Sheila determined to go through the 3rd Age Club to hassle me. Are you sure it's December the twenty-second, and not Friday the thirteenth?'

Chapter Fourteen

Denny and Vanessa lived in a modest semi off Doncaster Road, about a mile towards the town centre from The Lazy Luncheonette, and unlike Joe but in common with most working folk, they rarely crawled out of bed before eleven o'clock on Sunday morning. In this final run-up to Christmas, many people had abandoned the Sunday morning lie-in, but the Dixons were not amongst that number, as Joe discovered when he rang the doorbell at midday, and Denny answered still wearing his pyjamas and bathrobe.

'Tanked up last night, Joe,' he explained, running stubby fingers through his tousled hair. 'What do you want?'

'To talk to your missus.'

Joe had never fitted the template of lazing around in bed for half the morning. He was so accustomed to crawling out of bed in the early hours, that he was always up anyway, even on a Sunday, and with the threat of the extraordinary meeting hanging over him, he was keen to catch up on those problems he'd left in abeyance. Speaking to Van Dixon was one of them.

Mercifully, she was fully dressed in a pair of tight-fitting jeans and a loose-fitting top. She was skimming through the Sunday tabloids and their accompanying magazines when Joe stepped into the modestly furnished front room.

At the age of thirty-seven, the same as a

husband, she was a good-looking woman in her own way. Slim, but not emaciated, with muscular thighs, clearly outlined by the way her skin-tight jeans clung to her legs. But the attraction ended with the mere physical. Her red hair, augmented by a freckled skin, a mouth set in an almost permanent grimace, and eyes of green fire defied anyone, man, woman or mob, to challenge her.

The Dixons were childless by choice, and sitting opposite her, Joe could understand why. Vanessa had a reputation for selfishness, and Denny was interested only in his various appetites for food, drink, and other, less salubrious pastimes. In direct contrast to, say, Lee and Cheryl, neither of them would have made particularly good parents.

'So what do you want, Joe? Is it about our Tel?'

'Nope. It is about old Trelfus, but it's you I want to talk to.'

'I didn't know him.'

'Perhaps not, but you had an argument with him on the day you bought seventeen Kimbolton.'

Her eyes narrowed and Joe expected a barrage of verbal abuse. Just as quickly, the irritation subsided. 'Oh, was that him? I remember it. What about it?'

'I'm just making sure that you didn't go back in the early hours of the following morning to beat his brains in.'

This time, the temper did flash. She let loose a tirade of opinion, and did not stint on her choice of language. Joe was not certain that he understood all words she used to describe him, but he allowed the barrage of vernacular to settle before expanding on his initial challenge.

'You're wasting your breath, Vanessa. I know you. I remember you when you were a kid and you used to call in at the café for soft drinks. You were always mouthy then. Right now, I'm trying to keep your brother out of prison, and I had a tipoff that you'd been in an argument with Trelfus. You've just confirmed it. I'm speaking to everyone who was seen arguing with him around that time.'

Vanessa's temper was still simmering, bubbling away, ready to overflow at the slightest prompt. 'Yes, I did have a row with him. He accused me of murdering his daughter. I've never murdered anyone, I didn't know him and I didn't know his bloody daughter. So I told him where to go. Like I've just told you where you can get off.'

Joe frowned. 'Murdering his daughter? He didn't go into any more detail than that?'

Vanessa shook her head, her hair flouncing from side to side as she did so. 'Nope. I wasn't interested. I've more to do than listen to some wittering old scrote. And if you wanna know where I was on the night he was killed, I was right here, in bed, and Denny can vouch for that.'

Joe looked to her husband, who nodded. It meant little. Denny's fear of his wife was legendary, and if she had said she was busy putting on a striptease for the Sanford Regiment, he would have agreed.

Trelfus's accusation – if it were true – threw all of Joe's theories up in the air. How come

Gemma had never said anything about the murder of the old man's daughter?

The silent question bounced around his head, and he recalled his niece's story of Trelfus's granddaughter turning up at the station. Gemma had said she would send the woman to him, but she had not yet been in touch, and Sunday being a Sunday, especially three days before Christmas, it was unlikely that he would see her before the New Year.

His phone tweeted for attention, announcing a text message. He ignored it and focused his attention on the couple, at which point he realised Denny and Vanessa were waiting for him to say something. 'He definitely said that someone had murdered his daughter?'

'Definitely.'

'And he thought it was you?'

'Now you're getting the picture. Is that it? Only when that lazy bag of bones decides to move his fat, idle butt and get dressed, we have Christmas shopping to do.' She waved a shaking hand at her husband, identifying him as the "lazy bag of bones" in question.

'No. That's it.' Joe got to his feet. 'I'm not going to apologise for bothering you. I'm trying to clear your brother's name, and if you and Denny had been busy doing *something else*, I'd have still rung your doorbell.' He placed just enough meaning on the words "something else" to telegraph his meaning. 'I'll have to have a word with our Gemma, see what she can tell me. I'll be in touch.'

From there, Joe climbed into his car, and opened up the text message. It was from Brenda. *Meeting in progress. You're getting some stick. Where are you?*

He quickly put together a reply. *On my way.* After sending it off, he fired the engine, reversed into a nearby street, and turned left back towards The Lazy Luncheonette.

Three hundred yards down the road, he turned off, into the car park of the Miner's Arms, slotting his Vauxhall into a space alongside Brenda's Peugeot. As he climbed out, he noticed with some consternation, Martin's upmarket VW parked by the entrance to the bar. Martin was not a member of the 3rd Age Club, but if the meeting concerned Sheila and her illness and the allegations against Martin – as was almost certain – Joe was certain that her husband would be permitted to speak.

When he entered the top room, it was to find Stewart Dalmer on his feet, capitalising on the internecine divisions in the club.

'I've nothing particularly against Joe Murray,' Dalmer was saying. 'He's served this club well down the years, but this is not the first time he's let personal considerations impinge upon the membership, and I have to ask, is he the right man to take the Chair.'

As incumbent chairman, Tanner sat on the dais where Joe usually set up his disco equipment. In her capacity as club treasurer, Brenda sat to one side, and on the other, appearing weak, and shaky, was Sheila, the club secretary. Joe took a seat close to the dais, and Brenda cast a concerned glance at him. Sheila's look at his direction appeared more in anticipation of his potential downfall than his current welfare.

While Dalmer carried on in what was clearly a campaign speech – he was Joe's only rival in the forthcoming election for a new Chair – Joe cast a glance around the room.

Meetings were usually lively, often argumentative, but by and large, the membership got on well, and there was a good deal of joking. This time, the faces were grim, set hard, and it was impossible to guess how many would come down on his side. George Robson and his mate, Owen Frickley, stood at the rear of the room, propping up the bar. Alec and Julia Staines were in the middle, Mort Norris and his wife were off to one side, and behind them was Mavis Barker, who appeared as if she had already drunk her Sunday lunch. Tucked away in a corner, along with the Pyecocks and Cyril Peck, was Martin, as grim-faced as anyone else, his eyes straying constantly between Sheila, Brenda and Joe.

Dalmer finished his speech with a plea for the members to elect, 'someone who will set aside personal issues and put the club first.'

As he sat down, Tanner got to his feet. 'Right, ladies and gentlemen, we've heard from Mrs Naylor, we've heard from Mrs Jump, so I think the time is come to put matters to a vote. I need a couple of tellers and—'

Joe got to his feet and interrupted. 'Excuse me, Mr Chairman, but you haven't heard from me.'

'With respect, Joe, the meeting is about you.'

'And I'm not allowed to say anything in my defence? I've only been here a few minutes, and all I've heard is Stewart Dalmer campaigning for your job. If I was appearing in court, it would be my choice whether I spoke in my defence or not. You're not giving me a choice.'

From the back of the room, George Robson spoke up. 'Let Joe speak.'

A rhubarb murmur passed around the room, and once again, it was impossible to tell how many people were in favour or against. Paradoxically, it was Sheila who urged Tanner, let Joe have his say.

Unlike Dalmer, who had simply stood up by his seat, compelling many members to turn their heads and look at him, Joe moved to the front of the dais where everyone could see him.

'First, I must apologise for my late arrival. Other business prevented me getting here on time. I don't know what's been said, but it's obvious that at the core of the matter is this business of Sheila and my efforts to protect her life.' Another murmur ran round the room, and Joe gave it enough time to peter out before going on. 'It must be common knowledge that I'm suspicious of her husband, and for that, I *don't* apologise. But I need you to understand that I'm working as hard to prove Martin innocent as I am to prove him guilty. In other words, I'm sitting on the fence. If anything comes to light which shows me just how wrong I am, then I will apologise without reservation and in public to both Martin and Sheila.'

The years had granted Joe an ability to deliver a better than adequate speech on the spur of the moment, and he put that experience to good use, allowing a short pause to ensure there was sufficient stress on his next announcement.

'I'm being pilloried here for my concerns about a member's welfare. And not just any member but the woman who has acted as your secretary since the club was founded.'

The accusing shaft was not lost upon them. He could see it in their faces. But only George and Owen applauded, and rounded off with Owen's urge to, 'Make 'em have it, Joe.'

Almost immediately Martin was on his feet, his face crimson, his shaking finger pointing at Joe. 'You accused me of crimes I haven't committed.'

'Point of order, Mr Chair,' George called out. 'He's not a member of the club. He has no business saying anything.'

'Oh, shut up, you fat idiot.'

Fists clenching, George stepped forward, Martin turned to meet him, Les Tanner rapped for order, the low muttering of the members rose to a confused cacophony. Behind the bar, Eddie, the part-time barman, was already on the phone to the landlord.

'Gentlemen, please,' Tanner pleaded rapping his pen top loudly on the table.

He plea fell on deaf ears, and all hell was about to break loose.

With an irritated cluck, Joe raised his voice. 'Stop it. All of you. Owen, get between George and Martin. The rest of you, sit down and shut it.'

Order was gradually restored, landlord Mick Chadwick, appeared and after Eddie gave him appropriate reassurances, disappeared again, and the arguments reduced to odd murmurs, and Joe remonstrated with them.

'You're behaving like schoolkids. And you, Martin, owe George an apology. You wouldn't speak like that to one of your pupils.'

'No more than the apology you owe me.' As if to demonstrate that he was the bigger man, Martin faced George. 'My apologies, Mr Robson. I let my mouth run away with me.'

'Shove it.'

'I've told you once, George, knock it off,' Joe said. 'Martin has apologised and that should be an end of it.' He concentrated on Martin. 'And as for me owing you an apology, I don't. Not yet. To set the record straight, I have accused you of nothing. I asked you to explain certain suspicious aspects of your history, and as matters stand, you haven't explained them satisfactorily. When you do, *then* I will owe you an apology.'

Sheila stood unsteadily and as she spoke, Joe whipped his head to the left to look her in the eye. He regretted immediately. He had seen Sheila angry on many occasions, but now her face was filled with hatred. 'And you set about explaining those by breaking into my back garden, did you? Instead of asking? You decided to prove those by harassing my husband in class, while he was teaching? You set the police on his back and he explained the situation. If it's good enough for them, it should be for you, too.'

Joe's heart sank and he resumed his seat. 'I hope you think about that when you're in your box.'

Sheila was about to snipe again, but her anger overtook her and she had to sit down, gasping for breath.

Now Les Tanner prepared to have his say, but Brenda beat him to it.

'I want it on record that Joe was not alone. Rightly or wrongly, I was with him all the way, including during the so-called break-in at Mrs Naylor's. If you're going to lay any sanction on Joe, then I insist that you place them on me, too.'

Tanner took over. 'Thank you, Mrs Jump. What action to take – if any – is the main item of discussion. It's my feeling that as a friendly organisation we cannot simply overlook this matter, but do we agree or disagree with the actions of our friend and former Chair, Mr Murray?'

There were rumblings around the room and Joe distinctly heard someone say, '…should kick him out'. At the rear, George was still in heated and threatening debate with Martin. Looking around the familiar faces, he knew he could count on support from some quarters – Mavis Barker, Alec an Julia Staines, for example – but there others with whom he'd crossed swords over the years, and they would take a dimmer view of the last few days.

Without waiting for anyone to contribute to the proceedings, he stood up once again. 'You lot should make up your minds. In Cornwall, you were screaming because I didn't care, now you're screaming because I do.'

He marched towards the exit.

'Mr Murray… Joe…'

He turned to face the Chair. 'I'm sorry, Les, but I've already had enough of people slagging me off. Brenda, when you need a drink, I'll be downstairs.'

He marched from the room and made his way downstairs to the lounge bar, where he ordered a pint of lager.

'Send you to Coventry, have they?' Mick Chadwick asked as he pulled the beer.

'I don't know and I don't care, Mick. You do your best for them, and all you get for your trouble is a kick in the teeth.'

Mick took his money and rang up the sale. Handing over the change, he said, 'Tell me about it.' He waved a hand around the room. 'I'm best friends with this lot while I'm pulling pints, but you should hear the abuse when I get their change wrong.'

In no mood to listen to the landlord's complaints, Joe found an empty corner table, and sat mulling over the mess he had landed himself in. It was not the first time, and he was sure it would not be the last, but it was certainly one of the worst. Sheila had been at pains to point out that in all other instances, Joe fought a determined rearguard on behalf of accused members, but this time he was accusing… Well, not exactly accusing a member, but a man who was close to one.

He was not alone for long. With the meeting over, the members drifted into the lounge, or began to leave the pub. Brenda called at the bar and collected a drink, and then joined him.

'Censure motion,' she said. 'Against you, but I insisted they added my name to it.'

Joe grunted humourlessly. 'Les sitting on the fence again.'

'Not really, Joe. He's in your corner, but as Chair, he can't come out and say so. So he proposed a censure motion, which is one step short of suspending you, and only two steps the right side of kicking you out altogether. It's a means of expressing the membership's disapproval without taking more severe action.'

Joe watched Martin and Sheila leave the bar and climb into Martin's car. He brought his attention back to Brenda. 'I still insist we have it right. That man is too calm for someone facing this kind of allegation. He knows damn well we can't prove it. Not until he actually kills her, and by then, he'll have disappeared.'

Brenda slurped on a Campari and soda. 'What can we do? Sheila's all but disowned us, and you know what Gemma said. If we're not careful, we could be prosecuted.'

Joe took a large mouthful of his lager. 'I'd rather stand up and defend myself in court than do nothing and watch her die.' Even as he said it, Joe knew that there was no way they could narrow down their suspicions.

'Anything new on the Bailey-stroke-Trelfus business?'

'What?' Brenda's question brought Joe from his gloomy thoughts. 'Oh. No. Well, an argument with Van Dixon this morning, but it didn't amount to much. Old Trelfus accused her of murdering his daughter, and this was years ago. Complete twaddle.'

Brenda sighed. 'Why don't we just forget it all, Joe? Enjoy Christmas?'

'With a potential death sentence hanging over Sheila? I don't think so.'

Chapter Fifteen

The day before Christmas Eve saw The Lazy Luncheonette as crowded as ever, beginning in customary fashion with the flood of ravenous Sanford Brewery draymen.

But it was a surly, snappier Joe than unusual who greeted them. Christmas was less than forty-eight hours away, and he had more urgent matters than dealing with their banter.

He was equally churlish with his crew, snapping instructions for them, biting when they asked for clarification, and generally no fun to be around.

Brenda pulled him for it. 'You're taking it out on everyone, Joe, and it's not fair. It's not their fault Sheila tried to boot us out of the club.'

He took the lesson to heart, and made an effort to cool down, but the moment the morning rush was over, he was in his car, on his way to Gale Street, where he sat with his niece, and gave her a piece of his mind. 'Why didn't you tell me old Trelfus was accusing people of murdering his daughter?'

Like Brenda, Gemma was more than equal to it. 'Because I didn't know about it. Next question?'

Gemma's answer took the wind from his sails, and he frowned, his brow creasing, eyes narrowing, his mop of curly hair, reaching down towards the bridge of his nose.

'Hang on a minute. Trelfus is from Sanford, right? He claims his daughter has been murdered, yet the cops don't know about it? How many more unsolved murders do you have on your books?'

'To my certain knowledge, none. You helped to clear up most of them. Where did you get your information, and how good is it?'

'Van Dixon. I called to see her and Denny yesterday morning, because someone had seen or heard Van arguing with Trelfus the day before he was killed. She told me, he'd accused her of murdering his daughter. You know Van. She saw him off in no short order, and she didn't hang around to ask what he was talking about.'

Up to her eyes in paperwork, Gemma sighed. 'He was non-compos, Joe. I'm still trying to get hold of medical reports on him, but so far, all I've learned is that Social Services got a referral and he wouldn't have anything to do with them. He was an old man, probably confused, and what he really needed was the help he kept turning down. I'll look into it. The minute I have a minute. Now is that all, because I'd like to catch up this side of Christmas so I can take a couple of days off.'

'Just one other thing. You said his granddaughter had been giving you stick, and you were going to push her my way. I haven't seen anything of her.'

'I told her she'd find you in Galleries on Saturday. As far as I'm concerned, that was an end of it. I haven't seen or heard from her since.'

'You didn't tell her to check out Santa's Grotto?'

'No, I didn't.'

The penny dropped with Joe. 'And she's blonde, about thirty years old, isn't she?'

Gemma had heard her uncle put together facts so many times that she was not remotely surprised that he knew. 'Go on, then. Dazzle me.'

Joe smiled for the first time that morning. 'She tried everywhere in Galleries. Everywhere but Santa's Grotto.' He prepared to leave. 'All right, chicken, I'll leave you to it. Don't forget, open invitation to you and Howard any time over Christmas and New Year.'

He was in a slightly better frame of mind, as he drove back to The Lazy Luncheonette, but he was still puzzled over Trelfus's claim of a murdered daughter, and the police's lack of knowledge on the matter.

Although he was no closer to cracking the old man's killing, or the potential threat to Sheila's life, he was content with his morning's progress. He had brought it to Gemma's attention, and she would institute a search of the national database to see if Trelfus could be linked to any unsolved murders, albeit as a bereaved family member.

All around him, the streets of Sanford screamed Christmas, and very nearly brought Joe to boiling point. Never fond of Yuletide, this year it had taken a distinctly black turn, and as far as he was concerned, the sooner it was all over and done with, the sooner they went into the dark, dismal days of January, the happier he would be.

When he got back to the café, changed into his whites, it was to find Brenda bearing news. From the kitchen doorway, she angled a surreptitious finger towards the table by the main entrance. 'One blonde thirty-something for the use of. She'd been here about half an hour, and specifically asked to speak to you. I gave her a cup of tea and a toasted teacake, and told her you wouldn't be long. You'd better speak to her, Joe, before she clears off.'

A chubby woman, her face glowed with health, and Joe guessed that despite her excess weight, she took good care of herself. Her blonde hair was tied in a ponytail, and Joe couldn't help feeling that he'd seen her before. Something about the jowls, the prim set of her pursed lips, the beginnings of a double chin, and the sharp, blue eyes staring over the rim of for cup. He noticed that her ring finger was adorned with jewellery, amongst it, a gold wedding band.

Pouring two beakers of tea, he strode across to her and sat down.' Joe Murray. I believe you've been looking for me.' He pushed one beaker across to her, and they shook hands.

'Lucy Emerson,' she introduced herself. 'The police told me you were the man to speak to about my grandad's death. I was all over this rotten town on Saturday looking for you, and some woman in a shop told me that this was your place.'

'Every square inch of it,' he confirmed with an encouraging smile. 'Lucy – you don't mind if I call you by your first name, do you? – Lucy, I don't know what the police have told you, but I have been making enquiries, and quite frankly, I'm no nearer a solution than they are. Someone was in your grandfather's house that night, but we don't know who. It's also beginning to look as if his death may have been more of an accident.'

Lucy shook her head, the ponytail wagging from side to side as she did. 'Someone pushed him. That's what the police told me. That, Mr Murray—'

'Please call me Joe.'

'That, Joe, is manslaughter. Someone should be held to pay for that. I can't just let it go.'

Joe sympathised. 'I'm in total agreement with you, but from all DI Craddock has told me, there's a mass of forensic evidence, and none of it points in any particular direction. You don't mind if I speak honestly, do you?'

'You're going to tell me that my grandad was a miserable, bad-tempered old sod. I already know it. A lot of people think he was just off his trolley, but he wasn't. He was in full charge of his faculties, but he had anger issues.'

He could see the pain in her eyes. Never speak ill of the dead was probably good etiquette, but of absolutely no use in a murder (or manslaughter) investigation.

Joe made an effort at diplomacy. 'I never met him, Lucy, so I don't know, but the picture you just painted is the one I get from other people.' He delivered a lopsided smile. 'I can't criticise. If you want grouchy, you should see me first thing on Monday morning.'

Lucy cradled her beaker in both hands. 'Grandad had good cause. The police never got to the bottom of my mother's death.'

Her announcement reminded Joe of his visit to Vanessa Dixon. 'Ah. Right. This has been mentioned to me before. I've just come from the police station and checked with them, and they don't have many unsolved ...' He almost used the word "murders" but checked himself. '... suspicious deaths.'

Lucy sniffed disdainfully. 'Typical plod. Sorry. The woman I spoke to at the police station told me that she was your niece.'

Joe drank a mouthful of tea, allowing her a moment to calm down. 'You want to tell me about your mum and what happened to her?'

A misty look came over the woman's face and as she spoke, her eyes sparkled with the threat of tears. 'She was a lovely woman. My dad treated her badly, and then in the end, she threw him out. If I didn't know different, I'd swear blind it was him who killed her, but I do know different. She was on her own for about five or six years, and then she took up with another man. A hell of a nice guy... so we all thought. Grandad and me, we were really happy for her, she was the happiest I never seen her. She had a heart problem, and she was on regular medication for it. As long as she didn't overdo things, she was in no danger. Then, about four years ago, she had a heart attack. We'd been worried about it for a long time, me and Grandad.' A wistful smile played upon her lips. 'Everybody thinks Grandad was a miserable old sod, but not when he came to visit us, he wasn't. He loved his daughter, and he loved me. Anyway, Mum came home, and she was fine for a couple of weeks, but then she had a second heart attack. That was it. She was dead.'

As she spoke on, an awful feeling of déjà vu came over Joe.

'We had no problem with it, but what Mr nice guy did next was appalling. He took her insurance, and without even asking, put the house up for sale. We can do anything about it, obviously, but when he sold it, he took every penny for himself, and disappeared.'

Joe was trembling.

'Then, while later… maybe a year, maybe two, maybe less, I can't remember, the police got an exhumation order, and took her up. There'd been no post-mortem, you see, because she'd been in hospital just two weeks before her death. Anyway, they carried out an autopsy, and it concluded that she'd been poisoned by the very drugs that were supposed to keep her alive.'

Joe was not certain he could control his voice. 'And that was atropine. Wasn't it?'

All trace of emotion left Lucy's face, superseded by amazement. 'How did you know?'

'I need the answer to two questions. Your mother's name, and where did all this happen?'

'Deirdre Ullsworth, and it was in Ripon. Where I come from. Where Grandad came from. He moved down to Sanford sometime after the war, because there was no work in Ripon. I think he spent some time in places like Leeds, Bradford, Wakefield and Pontefract before he moved here. You see, Mr Murray, Grandad wasn't as bad as he was painted. The real bad people were Mum's partner, and the woman he'd been with before her. Some French redhead... or should I say a redhead who pretended to be French. She was the one who killed mother. I'm sure of it.'

Joe was struggling to keep his excitement under control. 'If I showed you photographs, could you identify this man?'

She shrugged. 'Hard to say. Same goes for the woman. We never actually saw her, but Grandad had seen her picture in the paper when she was supposed to have disappeared seven or eight years earlier.'

'Mervyn Nellis and Francine Varanne, only he was living with your mother under the name of Marlon Newman.'

Once again, Lucy was astonished. 'How did you know?'

'Believe it or not, I'm looking into the matter for North Shires Insurance, the people who paid out on your mother's death. It's one of two cases I'm investigating, and until you told me just now, I didn't realise they were linked.' Joe took out his phone, accessed the photo gallery, and scrolled through the pictures until he came to one of Martin and Sheila. He opened it, laid the phone on the table, and turned it to face Lucy. 'Is that Marlon Newman?'

She fell into silent, intense thought, scrutinising the image, trying to make up her mind. 'It looks like him, true, but I can't be sure. Bear in mind, it's a few years since I've seen him, and he had a beard when he was living with Mum.' She gave the phone back to him. 'It's not him you should be looking for. It's her. His tarty piece. If you could find her, she'd identify him.' She looked into Joe's eyes. 'You don't think he's living in Sanford, do you?'

'I do. What's more, I think he's targeting his next victim.' Joe brought his jackrabbit thoughts under control. 'Where are you staying, Lucy?'

'I'm not. I came to Sanford on Saturday morning to see the police, and they put me onto you, and I spent the afternoon looking for you. When I couldn't find you someone told me about this place, so I went home, and I drove here this morning.' She cast a glance at her wristwatch. 'Yes, I'll have to think about getting back. I have a husband and two children to think about. My mother-in-law's looking after the kids while I'm here.'

'Right. Fair enough. Before you go anywhere, you need to go back to the police station. I'll come with you, and trust me, Gemma will listen to you this time. But we have to move quickly... before he murders someone else.'

Lucy reluctantly agreed, and Joe gave Brenda a brief overview before throwing off his whites once again, leading the younger woman out through the back door, to the parking area where he climbed into his Vauxhall, and she jumped into her Fiat, and followed him.

Twenty minutes later, they joined Gemma in her office, and she listened to Lucy's expanded tail. At length, she took a formal statement from the young woman, and allowed her to go on her way. 'If anything comes of this, Mrs Emerson, we'll be in touch, but we may need you to come back to Sanford to identify them. But for now, you can go.'

As Lucy left, Gemma concentrated on Joe.

'It's not enough, Joe. She couldn't identify Naylor from your photograph, and if we pull him in again, he'll have us for harassment.' She chewed her lip agitatedly. 'What we really need, is a line on this Frenchwoman, this Francine Varanne. I don't know how many French nationals we have living in Sanford, but I'll bet it's more than one or two.'

A light bulb lit in Joe's head. 'You're probably right. But I know where I can find a French-speaking woman.'

He got to his feet and as he hurried out Gemma called after him. 'Where the hell are you going?'

'I'll be back later. Just trust me. This is your Uncle Joe speaking.'

And with that, he was gone.

Chapter Sixteen

Not for the first time Joe cursed the nose to tail traffic on the main roads in and out of Sanford. It seemed to him that while he was in a hurry, everyone else was happy to take their time. It was, after all, just two days to Christmas, and many people were already enjoying time off work. So why should they rush?

And when he eventually pulled up outside the long, white painted hut, it was to find the place locked up for Christmas.

There was a phone number on the notice to one side of the entrance. Hands shaking, partly from the cold, partly from the urgency, the need to get this case closed as quickly as possible, he punched in the numbers, and made the connection.

'Archie Hepple.'

'Archie. It's Joe Murray. I know you've shut down for Christmas, but I need to speak to your missus. Urgently.'

In stark contrast to the determination and assuredness of the auctioneer, Archie was pleasant and contingent. 'Come to the house. We're not going anywhere until Boxing Day... And even then, it's only a bit of shopping. You know where we live? Leeds Road. The house on the corner of Lingwell Street. You can't miss it, and you'll see the cars parked in the front yard.'

Joe checked his watch. Two o'clock. 'I'll be there in fifteen minutes.'

He jumped back into his car, and tore away from the auction room, spinning the car round further along the little industrial estate, and accelerating back to the main roads. Once again, traffic hampered him. If he'd been half as paranoid as all Billy Trelfus appeared to be, he would swear that the cars, vans, lorries, buses were deliberately trying to hold him up. And while he waited in the traffic, he broke the rule of a lifetime, and accessed the web on his mobile.

For many seconds, he fooled around seeking the correct site, and then dreaming up something he could put into it. A blast from a horn behind, brought him to his senses. Up ahead the traffic had moved on fifty yards. He put the car into gear, and accelerated quickly to catch up.

The hold-up was created by a recalcitrant set of traffic lights at a five-way junction another hundred yards ahead, lights which took an age between changes. Joe took advantage of the delay to complete his work on the Internet, and then looking at the results, rehearsed the phrase time and time again. By the time he reached the lights, and stopped again at the head of the queue, he was word perfect… Well, as perfect as he could be in an unfamiliar language.

Speeding along Leeds Road, driving past the block of flats where he lived, he picked out the Hepples' house from a distance of a hundred yards. A three-storey, Victorian/Edwardian edifice, complete with stone bay windows and a large open yard at the front, where Archie's Ford and his wife's Renault were parked.

Parking in Lingwell Street, Joe hurried to the front door, part of his mind contemplating the similarities and disparities between himself and Archie. Joe had inherited his business from his father, and likewise Archie. Joe had no clue on the size of the auction room's turnover, but he imagined it would be comparable with The Lazy Luncheonette. And yet, Archie lived in this grand mini-mansion while Joe, even allowing for its temporary nature, inhabited a council flat and was preparing to move into nothing more grandiose than a terraced house.

Telling himself that it was irrelevant, that he had never been one for the fripperies and trappings of an above-average income, he rang the doorbell, and a few seconds later, Archie opened up and invited him in.

A day off, and the auctioneer had dispensed with his usual business suit, preferring instead a pair of baggy jeans and a loose-fitting sweater. He greeted Joe amiably, and showed him through to a large kitchen/diner at the rear of the house, where Frankie was mulling over the morning newspapers over a cup of strong, black coffee.

Like her husband, she was casually attired. Her hair, which had been carefully brushed into place when he saw her at the auction room, was mussed, in a state of disarray, as if she had just got out of bed (which was possible), and she, too, wore a loose top, and a pair of white slacks.

She looked up and beamed a smile on Joe. 'Archie said you wanted to see me.'

Joe took out his phone and enunciated

carefully. '*Je benen vallen eraf.*'

Frankie laughed but a frown crossed her forehead. 'I'm sorry, Joe. I don't understand.'

'Okay. Suppose I said…' Joe checked his phone again, and in a poor imitation of a French accent, said, '*Tes jambes tombent.*'

She laughed again, more nervously this time. 'My legs are falling?'

Joe took a seat opposite her. 'According to the Internet it should translate as "your legs are falling off". But that's not the point, Frankie. The point is you didn't understand when I said it in Dutch, and yet you claim to come from Knokke-Heist. According to my research, Knokke-Heist is in Northeast Belgium, not far from Zeebrugge, and it's a Flemish community. I'm not saying they wouldn't understand French, but they predominantly speak Dutch.' Joe was satisfied with the way her colour drained and the shock crossed her face. 'Now don't you think it's time you told me the truth about Francine Varanne.'

For one horrible moment, Joe worried that he had pushed too far. She almost swooned, and her hands leapt to her breast, as if the mention of the name had given her palpitations.

Archie, his normally pleasant features now a mask of concern, hurried to the sink, for a glass of water, and gave it to her. She gulped a mouthful down, hiccupped, and set the glass shakily on the laminate table.

Joe, confident that she was all right, pressed his case. 'Billy Trelfus must have recognised you when you knocked on his door. And you recognised him, didn't you? The woman who murdered his daughter. That's why you never dare knock again.'

She shook her head. 'No. No, Joe. You've got it wrong.'

Joe relaxed. He was on the final stretch, and his concern for Sheila's welfare was receding with every passing moment. 'In that case, put me right.'

She took her time regaining her composure, drank from the glass again, her shaking hands now under better control, and for a few moments, she stared through the rear window at the grave, miserable day beyond.

'It's true that the old man did recognise me, and yes, he accused me of killing his daughter. "You and that Newman". Those were his precise words. I didn't know what he was talking about, but a few days later, the old fool managed to get the story into the Sanford Gazette, and they syndicated it to one or two national dailies. That's when I panicked. That's when I decided I could never go near him again. He'd seen the redhead woman who murdered his daughter, but he was wrong. I had nothing to do with his daughter's death, but the piece in the papers carried a photograph of the poor woman and her partner, Marlon Newman. I recognised him right away. When I was married to him, he was Mervyn Nellis.' The first hint of tears sparkled in her eyes. 'He was the man who tried to murder me almost ten years before.'

The announcement drew Joe up short. A few minutes previously, his concerns for Sheila's welfare had all but disappeared. He had Billy Trelfus's killer, he had Deirdre Ullsworth's murderer, Martin Naylor was (in all probability) innocent. Now Frankie had thrown a fresh spanner in the works. All bets were off.

'Keep talking,' he insisted.

'What can I tell you? You've already worked out that I'm Francine Varanne, and French by birth. I met Mervyn Nellis when he was on holiday in the area where I grew up, the Dordogne. I came from a town called Bergerac and we met when I was on a day trip to Bordeaux, where he was staying. He was charming, gentle, fun to be with, and it was a case of love at first sight. Three months later we were married, and I agreed to come to England... Darlington. I spoke good English, and France was only a couple of hours away by air. It was a good time. Everything in the garden was wonderful, as the English say.' She drank more water, and held out the glass for Archie to refill. When he had done so, she went on. 'It didn't take long for matters to turn sour. I have expensive tastes.' She gave a humourless little laugh. 'Ask Archie. He'll tell you.' She held her husband's hand. 'Mervyn wasn't as tolerant as this lovely man, and fights were frequent. They got so bad, so noisy that the neighbours complained. And then, suddenly, I became ill. Stomach troubles. I couldn't understand it. I have a stomach of cast iron, I never, never have problems of that nature. And then one day, I happened to see him adding something to my food. I don't know what it was. Washing-up liquid, bleach, disinfectant. Even real, genuine poison. I don't know, but it was enough for me. I left him. Ten minutes after seeing what he was doing, I was out of the door, and gone. I had no clothing with me, and not much money, and I daren't use a cash machine for fear that he might be able to track me down. So I phoned Papa, and he wired money to me. Enough to get me on a ferry to Zeebrugge, where he picked me up, and drove me down to Bergerac. And there I stayed, in hiding for the next seven years.'

Joe was slightly puzzled. 'Why come back to England?'

Her worried features became angry. The colour returned to the cheeks, and when she next spoke, her voice was reduced to something not much more than a virulent hiss. 'He had me declared dead. The insurance, you see. Fifty thousand pounds worth. Not to mention whatever equity there was in the house. We only found out when the authorities contacted my family again to ask whether they'd seen anything of me. Mama and Papa were under strict instructions to deny having seen me, and when my father told them as much, they said that I would be declared officially dead.' She sighed and began to calm down. 'There are advantages to being dead, Joe. It meant I could return to England without arousing suspicion, and that's what I did. Naturally, by the time I got to Darlington, everything was all done and dusted and Mervyn Nellis had disappeared without trace.'

'And yet, you didn't go to the police.'

'I thought about it, but I could see which way it would go. Mervyn had gone. There was no trace of him. It seemed to me that the police would take the attitude that he and I had worked in collusion to rip off the insurance company.'

Joe considered the proposition and found it to his liking. Not only would the police have suspected her of collusion, but it would have made her presence public, and that would bring out the threat of Mervyn Nellis once again. 'But you didn't go back to France, did you?'

Frankie shook her head. 'I like England. I'd always like England. And while I was here, there was always the chance that I might bump into Mervyn, and would I make him pay. There wasn't much work in Darlington, so I made my way to Leeds, and took a job in a supermarket. A year later, I met Archie, we fell in love and... Well, the rest is history.'

Questions tumbled about Joe's head. 'You speak with an excellent Yorkshire accent.'

Frankie threw back her head and laughed. That was more like the woman Joe was familiar with. A woman who enjoyed life. 'Constant practice,' she said. 'And I could have got away with it for years yet, if you hadn't come poking your nose in.'

'Knokke-Heist?'

She shrugged. 'One of those places I saw signposted when Papa picked me up in Zeebrugge. It never occurred to me that they were Flemish speaking, but it was an adequate cover story... At least until today.'

'So let me get this straight, Frankie. You're saying that Billy Trelfus had it all wrong, and it was your husband who murdered his daughter, not you.'

'I promise you, my friend, I had nothing to do with it, and I don't know where he got the idea from, unless the police somehow tied her death to my disappearance.'

Joe knew immediately how it had happened. Eliot Banks. He was the man who had made the initial connection, and it was practically certain that the police would have shown Billy Trelfus photographs of Mervyn Nellis, and those photographs would very likely have included Frankie. Given Billy's capacity for misunderstanding, he would have assumed that Marlon Newman and Frankie were working together, but having met Marlon, he would not believe that such a mild-mannered, friendly man could carry out cold-blooded murder. Therefore, it could only be Frankie.

Joe took out his smartphone, opened up the image gallery for the second time that day, and scrolled to a photograph of Martin Naylor. He turned it to face Frankie.

'Is that Mervyn Nellis?'

She took the phone from him and studied the image. 'It looks like him, but the nose isn't right. Mervyn had a hook nose, a – what do you call it? – Roman nose. This man's nose is straight.' She handed the phone back. 'I'd have to speak to him to be certain, but that's never going to happen.'

'Why not?'

'Because I don't want any of this to come out, Joe. When I first came back to this country, I was prepared to face him, expose him. But when I learned how he'd murdered Billy's daughter, I suddenly realised how dangerous he was. If he finds me, he'll finish what he started all those years ago.' She urged him to understand. 'Think about the auction house. Think about the way you never see me.'

Joe shrugged. 'I wouldn't know. I've never been to one of your auctions.'

'You don't know what you're missing. During the sales, I keep a deliberately low profile. That's why Billy could never find me again after the one time I knocked on his door. And while I keep that low profile, it's fairly certain that Mervyn will never find me.'

'We can get you protection, Frankie,' Joe said. 'Listen to me. I'm giving you the benefit of the doubt and assuming that you're telling the truth. I think that Mervyn, Marlon, Martin, call him what you like, is right here in Sanford, and is about to kill again. I may be wrong. It may be that the man I've just show you is completely innocent. But you, Frankie, are the only one who could possibly identify him.'

She shied away. 'I understand what you're saying, Joe, and I'm sorry, but the answer is no.'

Joe turned to Archie, appealing for his help, but the auctioneer shook his head. 'Sorry, Joe, but I stand by what Frankie's said. Face it, we're getting old. All of us. We'd be no match for this barmpot.'

Joe struggled to control his frustration. 'All right. I'll have to pass on what you've told me to the police. But they'll want to speak to you, and I guarantee they'll put a lot more pressure on you than I can. In the meantime, try and have a good Christmas… with one eye over your shoulder.'

Perhaps it was the last half dozen words, but Joe had barely reached the room door when Frankie called him back. 'All right. Let me follow you to the police station, and I'll speak to them.' She looked up at her husband. 'But only if Archie can be with me.'

Joe smiled. 'I'm sure Gemma won't mind.'

He went ahead, fighting yet again with the increased traffic the crowded streets, the packed multi-storey car park in Galleries, and almost thirty minutes passed before he sat with his niece, and told her what he had learned.

She listened, occasionally making notes, and eventually said, 'I'll take a statement from Frankie, sure, but if she can't identify Martin from your photograph, we're still all at sea.'

'Yeah, well, I've been thinking about that. All the money he had, it wouldn't have had been too difficult to get a nose job, would it?'

Gemma frowned. 'Can you do that? Have your nose straightened?'

'I think so. Surgeons straighten out boxers' noses when they get broken, don't they? And other people have nose jobs to help with breathing problems. I think it's called rhinoplasty.'

Archie and Frankie arrived about ten minutes after Joe, and after words of reassurance from Archie, Gemma took Frankie into an interview room, where the auctioneer's wife would give a full account of her history, the same one she had given Joe. In the meantime, Joe and Archie repaired to Ma's Pantry in Galleries, and over a cup of tea, the discussion naturally turned to Christmas and the New Year.

Joe was not surprised to learn that Archie was as hostile to the season as him.

'The first wife left me in the run-up to Christmas, and it's never been the same since. Scampered. Slung her hook with an estate agent from Sheffield. Left me high and dry with a seventeen-year-old daughter to look after.'

'Still, you seem to be well settled with Frankie.'

'She's a good lass, Joe. Her tastes aren't as expensive as she likes people to think, and she takes good care of me. And she gets on well with Ros.'

'That's all that matters then, Archie. So will you be working over the Christmas period?'

Archie laughed showing yellowed, nicotine-stained teeth. 'Not bloody likely. The day after New Year we're jumping on a plane and flying off to Lanzarote for a couple of weeks.'

Joe found himself in complete sympathy with the auctioneer. He often wondered why he didn't take advantage of the lower prices in January.

'The weather's not scorching hot,' Archie was saying, 'but it's warmer and drier than Sanford, and you can still get decent British beers there.'

'Yeah, I know. My ex-missus lives in Playa de Las Américas. Tenerife. I've often thought…'

Joe trailed off as mobile phone warbled for

attention. He checked the menu window, read "Brenda" and excusing himself to Archie, made the connection.

'Joe, where the hell are you?' Her voice sounded urgent and distressed.

'Police station. Frankie Hepple's giving a statement, I'm with Archie, lending moral support. What's the matter?'

'Sheila. I've just had a call from Les Tanner. She rang him because, obviously, she's not speaking to us. She's taken a turn for the worse, Joe. Les and Sylvia went round there, and they called an ambulance for her. She's been rushed into hospital.'

Chapter Seventeen

By the time Joe got to Sanford General Hospital, Brenda was already sat with Tanner and Sylvia in a small ante-room towards the rear of the A & E department. Joe recalled the place well. He had been rushed to this same area of the hospital when he had a faux heart attack a couple of year previously, and he guessed that Sheila and Brenda had waited in this same room most of the night, waiting for news.

Les was unstinting in his praise for both Brenda and Joe. 'Considering Sheila's vitriol against you yesterday, it's pleasing to see the flame of genuine friendship hasn't completely died.'

In his less charitable moments Joe was convinced that Les, an avid reader of biographies, especially those of well-known military figures, collected such aphorisms and stored them in his head, awaiting only the perfect moment to use them.

'You don't throw fifty years away, Les, on the basis of one argument. Even if she did accuse us of burglary.'

Brenda supported Joe's opinion. 'Even though we really were burgling her back garden, I'm sure she knows deep down that we did it with her welfare in mind.'

Joe took a chair alongside her and concentrated on the other couple. 'So what happened? Do we know?'

Les would have spoken up, but Sylvia had decided that if anyone was going to tell the tale, it would be her. 'She rang about three o'clock. Oh, she was in a terrible state. She could hardly breathe. Naturally, Les and I went round there right away. She only lives a few streets away, if you remember. She was nauseous, vomiting, confused, and the smell… oh, dear me. I can't begin to describe it. Awful.'

'And where was Martin?' Joe demanded.

'Out,' Sylvia replied. 'We don't know where. Even Sheila didn't know where he was, which is why she rang us. We tried ringing him, but his phone is off. Eventually, Les decided she needed medical help and sent for the paramedics. They ordered the ambulance and here we are.'

'They don't know what's wrong,' Brenda said, and Joe guessed she had asked the questions before he arrived. 'They have her in a private room on the strength of her medical insurance, and all they're saying is it's some kind of gastric problem.'

'Poisoning.'

Les tried to remain good humoured as he warned Joe. 'Now come on. We had all that yesterday. There's absolutely nothing to say—'

'I have more information now, Les, and there's good reason to suppose that Brenda and I had it half right. Someone has been trying to poison Sheila.' He scowled. 'I'm just not sure who.' An idea occurred to him and he leaned into Brenda. 'Do you still have a key for Sheila's place?'

'Forget it.'

'No. I mean it. If Martin isn't there, we need to find him, and anyway, I need to bring you up to speed on the things I've learned.'

'It's not advisable, Joe,' Les warned.

Joe held his patience. 'Listen to me, all of you. It's entirely possible that Martin is already dead, and Sheila is the final target.'

His alarming and unexpected announcement sent a shock of consternation through them.

'I may be wrong,' he went on. 'I hope I am. But it needs to be checked out. The only way I can do that is by going to Sheila's place and letting ourselves in.'

Sylvia laughed nervously. 'Joe, we were there. He wasn't.'

'And you checked every room, did you? All due respect, Sylvia, but he could have been lying dead in another room, and if Sheila was as confused as you say, she may not have been any the wiser.'

Brenda's worry flooded to the surface. 'Are you serious?'

'When it comes to something like that, I'm not likely to be joking, am I?'

'All right let's find out.' Brenda smiled at Les and Sylvia as she got to her feet. 'We'll be back as soon as.'

'We'll hang on here,' Les said. 'Keep us informed.'

They headed out to Joe's car, and as they settled in and he started the engine, he went into a long, detailed explanation of the afternoon's events.

It had occurred to him only when Les and Sylvia confirmed Martin's absence, and Sheila's lack of knowledge of his whereabouts. He had only a vague idea how Frankie could have done it, but he was now convinced that she had lured Martin away and murdered him, gone back to Sheila's bungalow, poisoned her, and then made her way home in time to meet with Joe.

And as he related the tale, he recalled Frankie's appearance when he arrived at the Hepples' home. She took pride in her appearance, and he had never seen her so dishevelled, especially in relation to her hair. Had it been mussed in a struggle with Martin? It was entirely possible.

By the time he had finished explaining his theory, they were almost at Larch Avenue, and Brenda was dumbfounded.

'So now, instead of prosecuting Martin, we're looking to save his life?'

'If I'm right, Brenda, I think we're probably too late.'

He pulled up outside Sheila's place, killed the engine and they hurried to the main door, at the side of the house. The place was in darkness and so was the doorway, and Brenda fumbled through her purse for the key. As close friends, both of them living alone, she and Sheila had had keys for each other's houses for many years, but she could not recall any time when she'd had to use it.

She found the key, and aimed it at the lock,

but a shaking hand made her message twice on the trot. Joe, in better control of his nerves, took it from her, slotted it into the lock, turned it, threw the door open.

Like Brenda, he was familiar with Sheila's home. As they stepped over the threshold, he automatically reached up to his right and switched on the hall lights. Brenda hurried through to the living room and kitchen, while Joe burst into the master bedroom, and found it empty. He checked the second, smaller bedroom, with the same result, and the bathroom proved similarly devoid of life.

Returning from the living room, where she had found no trace of Martin, Brenda entered the master bedroom, and with her nerves on edge, her entire arms trembling, slid open the wardrobe door. Joe joined her and what they saw chilled both of them to the bone.

Taking up one complete wall, all the way to the windowsill, the right-hand half, the side closest to the window, sported Sheila's clothing: dresses, suits, blouses, jumpers even jogging pants and at floor level, shoes and trainers. On the upper shelves were neatly folded sheets, duvet covers, pillow slips, a couple of wool blankets and spare pillows.

The left half was barren. Not one item of Martin's clothing hung there, when Brenda checked the dresser, where Sheila stored their underwear, she could find plenty of her best friend's smalls, but…

'Not one single pair of shreddies. Not even a jockstrap.' She turned an angry face on Joe. 'He's done a bunk.'

Joe cursed, and Brenda had to warn him about his language. 'I'm sorry. But I had it right the first time, and I let this afternoon with Frankie fool me into thinking different. Come on. We'd better lock up and get back to the hospital. I'll ring Gemma on the way and tell her what's what.'

'You drive. I'll ring Gemma.'

She made the call, Brenda put the phone on speaker, and Gemma surprised them both by announcing that she was already ahead of them. 'I had the groom's speech from their wedding on my laptop,' she explained. 'When I played it to Frankie Hepple, she confirmed that it was the voice of Mervyn Nellis, and we're betting that he was also Marlon Newman. I've got an all ports warning out on him. Where are you two now?'

'On our way back to the hospital,' Brenda said. 'Sheila is not gonna take this well, and I've a feeling she'll need Les, Sylvia, and the pair of us.'

The evening traffic was no thinner than it had been during the daytime, and as he crawled along, Joe picked up on Brenda's last announcement. 'What she needs right now is a police guard. If Naylor realises that she's not dead, he might just go for her in the hospital.'

'I'll get a couple of bodies down there,' Gemma agreed and terminated the call.

Joe's opinion caused Brenda more worry. 'You don't think he would, do you, Joe? Go for her in the hospital, I mean.'

'He doesn't have much to lose, Brenda. We're onto him, the cops are onto him. If either of us gets to him, he's going down for life, but if he can get rid of Sheila, he might still get away with it. Our testimony is mainly opinion and it won't count for much.' He made a sharp left onto York Road, and the vast spread of the hospital buildings appeared half a mile ahead of them. 'In any case, he's a serial wife-killer. If he didn't manage to bump her off, he'd consider it a failure.'

A couple of minutes later, he pulled into the hospital car park, and as they cruised along the parallel lanes looking for a space, Brenda spotted a familiar VW saloon.

'Oh my God. That's Martin's. He's here.'

Joe came to full alert, accelerated to the end of the parking lane, turned right, and right again, bringing him to the main entrance of the hospital, where he jammed on the brakes, killed the engine, and got ready to climb out.

'Call Gemma. Tell her he's here and she needs to send in the heavy mob. I'll get in there and stop him if I can.'

He leapt from the car and a security attendant waylaid him. 'Hey, you can't park there.'

Taking a leaf from Lee's book, Joe shouldered him out of the way and rushed into the hospital, weaving through crowds of staff, visitors and patients, hurrying to the A & E Department, where many amazed eyes turned on him.

He burst into the anteroom, where Les and Sylvia were still waiting.

'Martin. Have you seen him?'

Both frowned in puzzlement. 'No.'

Joe rushed back out, and looked both ways

along the corridor. It was punctuated with doors here and there, and he had no clue where Sheila was.

He sensed Les behind him, but he could not wait. When a nurse appeared from one room, he collared her. 'Mrs Riley... I mean, Mrs Naylor. Where is she?'

'I beg your pardon. Who are you?'

'I don't have time to faff about, girl. She's in danger. Where is she?'

'I really don't think—'

'I'm not asking you to think. Just tell me where she is.'

His urgency permeated her regimented approach, and she pointed along the corridor. 'Room sixty-seven. She's very ill.'

Joe was already running. 'If I don't get a move on, she'll be dead.'

* * *

'Sheila.'

The voice was soft, tender, loving. A man's voice drifting in from somewhere far away. Peter? Was she to be reunited with her beloved husband after all these years?

From somewhere in the distance the sound of celebratory music reached her. She recognised it right away. *Hark the Herald Angels Sing*. One of her favourite carols.

Christmas. That special time of year: special to her, special to the Rileys as a family. The joy of giving, the joy of receiving, the joy of watching the two boys excitedly opening their presents after a visit from Santa.

Strange, amorphous visions came to her. Peter's smiling face, melding, blending quickly to the wizened, angry features of Joe Murray, and then to Brenda's laughing features as she knocked back a slug of Campari. There was another man, a smiling, good looking gentleman, and Sheila knew she should know him, but his name escaped her confused memory. Marlin? Marvin? No. Martin. That was it. Martin. Why was Martin there? If Peter saw the lusty way he was looking at her, there would be an argument.

'Come on, Sheila. Wake up. I've some medicine for you.'

Peter was a policeman not a doctor. How could he have medicine for her? Then she remembered. Peter had taken so many health and safety courses that he knew instinctively what was wrong with her and would know which medicine would be right.

'Wakey-wakey, sleepy-head. Time for your medicine.'

She felt her lips crease into a generous smile. It was definitely Peter, repeating the very words she had said so many times to Peter Jnr and Aaron when they were children.

Her eyes flickered open, and blurred reality greeted her. Peter was gone, but there was another special man here to take his place. Her smile softened, filling slowly with the glow of love. Real memories emerged from the depths of her mind. How could Joe Murray and Brenda Jump really imagine this wonderful man would do her any harm?

Martin reached an arm behind her pillow, brought her forward into a half-sitting position. 'The doctors gave me some medicine for you, Sheila.' He brought a glass phial towards her lips. 'You have to drink it.'

Anything. Anything to take away the pains, settle the internal mess that was her gastric system. She parted her lips. No matter how awful it tasted, if it helped…

And then she saw it.

It was nothing tangible, nothing anyone could get hold of and examine. Nothing a scientist, doctor, pathologist could analyse. It was something only a woman in love would notice. A gleam in his usually calm, adoring eyes. A hint of determination, of triumph, of victory… of madness.

Through the drug-induced haze of prescription medicines, the logic circuits of her mind began to mesh. She was in hospital. Doctors and nurses did not give medicines for relatives to administer.

And with that, the awful realisation struck her. Her closest friends, two of the people in this world dearest to her, two people she had castigated and disowned, had been right. This man did not love her. He craved only that which he could get his hands on when she was no more.

As the clear liquid came close to her lips, she raised an arm, and pushed his away. 'No.' She was weak. Her strength was gone, and the effort almost drained her completely. The voice sounded not like hers, but someone else, someone far away.

'Now, come on, Sheila. Don't argue. This is for your own good. It'll take away all your pain.'

He brought the phial to her again, and she gripped his wrist, pushing it away. The little strength she had was fading, and the outcome was inevitable. She began to cry, calling out for help in a voice so feeble that it barely reached her ears.

And the deadly liquid came closer and closer.

* * *

Joe's heart pounded in his chest. Hurtling along the corridor, he looked into every private room, desperately praying that he would be in time. Old men, old women, not so old women, young men, children, families... Where was she?

He almost shot past the room. He could see a doctor helping a patient, trying to feed her medicine. It was only as he ran by the door that he realised the patient was Sheila, and the doctor was no doctor. He burst into the room. The glass phial was within inches of Sheila's lips. She was putting up a fight, but she had no strength.

Joe Murray was not known for his fighting skill, but he had never lacked courage. His flat cap flying from his head, he hurled himself across the bed, landed on Sheila's legs. She whimpered feebly. Joe had no time to worry about her. Stretching out his arm, he knocked the bottle away. It flew from Martin's hand, struck the far wall down, near the skirting board, and shattered. The smell of household bleach reached Joe's nostrils.

Staggering back away from the bedside, Martin recovered quickly.

'Why can't you learn to mind your own business, Murray?' The normally pleasant tones of his voice were gone, replaced by frustrated anger.

Joe was wriggling to get off the bed, telegraphing an apology to Sheila with his eyes. Landing on her like that caused her frail features to twist in agony. Before he could get to his feet, however, Martin grasped him by the shoulders and flung him against the far wall. Joe crashed into the bare plaster and his shoulder screamed at him. He ignored it.

'The cops are on their way, Naylor. You won't get out of here.'

'In that case, I'll send you and her to Valhalla before they get me.'

Joe looked frantically around for a weapon. Nothing. Not quite nothing. On the bedside cabinet was a plastic jug, half full of water. He picked it up and threw it at the approaching menace.

It had little effect. Somewhere in mid-air, the lid flew off, and Martin was drenched, but it did not stop him coming forward.

And suddenly, Joe knew the fear of imminent annihilation. In the distance, he could hear the wah-wah sound of emergency vehicle sirens. Police rather than an ambulance, he hoped. They could not possibly make it in time to save him or Sheila. He drew in as deep a breath as his tortured lungs would allow, and mentally consoled himself with the thought that at least he had stopped this maniac murdering any more innocent men and women.

He closed his eyes expecting nothing but death… and without warning, the cavalry arrived.

With a loud crash and rattle, the door flew open. Brenda burst in, accompanied by the security guard who had warned Joe against parking by the Hospital entrance. Brenda kicked and connected with Martin's shin. He yelped and backed off half a yard. As he did so, the security guard leapt on him and brought him crashing to the floor.

There came the sound of running feet along the corridor. Doctors, nurses, and somewhere behind them, uniformed police officers, crowded into the room. Out in the corridor, Les Tanner, his face creased with concern, and Sylvia Goodson, a hand held to her open mouth, watched the chaotic scene unfold.

Somewhere amongst the melee, Joe was knocked to the floor, and sat in the corner, his back against the wall. Medics skirted the bed, their attention on Sheila, and the spilled liquid on the floor. The police wrestled furiously with Martin, pressed him face down to the composition floor tiles, and handcuffed him.

Brenda helped Joe to his feet, and they watched the efforts of the nurses trying to calm their patient. Struggling to regain her breath, her senses clearing, Sheila shooed them away, and turned tearful eyes on her two oldest friends. Like an injured puppy or cub seeking the security of the pack, she reached out her arms.

Brenda hugged her, and as she held the weeping woman, she smiled up at Joe. 'From now on, we'll have to call you just-in-time Joe.'

Chapter Eighteen

It was a tired and sore Joe Murray who crawled out of bed (in his own apartment) at five o'clock the following morning.

His shoulder was bruised where Martin had thrown him against the wall, and the tussle had aggravated the slight injury to his ankle he'd sustained in Sheila's back garden the previous Friday. But it was fatigue more than pain that troubled him the most. It was nine o'clock in evening by the time he and Brenda were through talking to the police and hospital authorities. They managed a bite to eat at the hospital cafeteria, after which, he dropped her at home, and then came back to his flat.

From then, the telephone had hardly stopped ringing. First it was Les Tanner, congratulating him on his "fortitude" and letting him know that he had already informed many of the 3rd Age Club members. Soon after, those members began to ring. George and Owen from the public bar of the Miner's Arms, Alec Staines talking to Joe while his wife, Julia, was on another phone to Brenda, then Howard calling from home to thank him for his efforts on his Aunt Sheila's behalf, and finally, sometime around eleven o'clock, it was the editor of the Sanford Gazette, Ian Lofthouse, asking for the full story. Joe gave him no more than an overview, and finally crawled into bed around half past eleven.

He had little choice but to put the night's events behind him. It was Christmas Eve. The draymen would be in for breakfast, and beyond them there would be a constant stream of customers until they closed the café's doors, which, as was customary, would be around noon so they could get away by two in the afternoon, allowing the staff time to get to Sanford for those last-minute Christmas bits and pieces. The very thought reminded Joe that he had not yet bought anything for Gemma or Howard, and like it or not, he would have to make yet another journey into town to deal with it.

When he got to The Lazy Luncheonette a little after six, Lee had already opened up, and he was in awe of his uncle. 'You're a hero, Uncle Joe. You stopped this toe rag from topping Auntie Sheila. You should get a medal.'

'It was something and nothing, Lee. Now, can we get on with breakfast? The brewery bananas'll be here in an hour, we'd all like to knock off early today.'

There was more to come. Brenda arrived just before seven o'clock, and greeted him with a grateful kiss. 'My hero,' she said. She had no more news from the hospital, and Joe had not yet heard from the police.

The biggest surprise of the morning came when the draymen began to arrive, and Joe learned that he was, indeed, lauded as a hero. Ian Lofthouse had already run the story on the Gazette's website, and it had been picked up by Radio Sanford, who as well as detailing a statement from the police, named Joe as the hero of the hour. It led to plaudits from the draymen, and more than one cynically humorous comment to the effect that Joe would probably increase his prices on the back of his fame.

As the morning progressed, more and more people congratulated him to such a degree that he began to tire of it. Brenda rang the hospital at half past ten, to be told that Mrs Naylor – now insisting that her name was Riley – had been sedated, had spent a comfortable night, and was recovering from whatever toxins Martin Naylor had fed her over the last few days, weeks, and months.

Half an hour later, Gemma rang, and after offering her congratulations to her uncle, told him that Naylor had been seen by a doctor, was declared fit to be interviewed. They were waiting for both the duty solicitor to turn up, and Chief Inspector Roy Vickers to get to Sanford from Wakefield, where he had planned nothing more than an idle final day before Christmas.

'We'll be interviewing him at three o'clock this afternoon, Uncle Joe,' Gemma concluded, 'and Chief Superintendent Oughton says you're welcome to sit in the observation room with him, if you wish.'

'I'll be there,' Joe promised.

At twelve noon, he locked up, and an hour later, after cleaning down and ensuring everything was secure for the next two days, he paid his staff, and the casuals, a twenty-pound Christmas bonus each, bagged up the takings, and everyone finally left, making an early start to the Christmas break.

'I'm going home first,' Brenda said. 'Then I'll be going to the hospital. I'll be there when you're finished at the police station, if you wanna catch up with me.' There was a wistful note to her voice. 'I think Sheila's going to need a lot of help to get over this.'

'I'll give it a coat of thinking about while I'm in Sanford, and catch you later.'

For the umpteenth time that week, Joe battled with the traffic, making his way into Sanford and the multi-storey car park in Galleries. He'd had plenty to eat during the day, and was happy to ignore the fare on offer at the mall's cafés. Instead, he visited one or two department stores, collected a moderately expensive bottle of perfume for Gemma, and a slightly cheaper aftershave for Howard, treated himself to a couple of CDs and DVDs, and with the time coming up to half past two, made his way across Gale Street to the police station.

Vickers greeted him with a slight air of consternation (they had never seen eye to eye) but nevertheless offered his thanks for Joe's intervention the previous night, and stressed that while Joe was welcome to observe, he would not be allowed to intervene in the interrogation process.

'You think he's gonna cough?' Joe asked.

'We think he'll plead diminished responsibility,' Gemma replied. 'It won't make much difference. If we can get everything out of him, he'll go down for the rest of his life.'

Joe smiled broadly. 'And there's me thinking

Santa Claus was just a fairy tale.'

* * *

'My real name is Maxim Anatoly Nikolayev. Officially, I'm Russian. I was born in Moscow, but my father was a member of the Soviet trade mission to Great Britain, and I came to this country when I was just a few months old. My birth certificate and passport are, as you've worked out, expensive, high quality forgeries. And that, Inspector, is why you were never able to trace me properly.'

With his solicitor alongside him, Martin faced the determined Vickers, who had charitably allowed Gemma to lead the early questioning.

'You told us you were born in York,' Gemma protested.

'No. I told you York was my hometown, which it was. It's where I made my base.'

In the observation room, sat alongside Don Oughton, Joe seethed. 'Does he expect us to believe that a baby could have escaped the Russians back then?'

It was almost as if Martin could hear him. 'I was less than a year old when my father decided he'd had enough of the Soviet Union, and he defected, bringing my mother and me into the care of the Foreign Office. He didn't have any great state secrets to hand over to the British or the Americans, and when they learned that, the Yanks lost interest. but the British accepted his defection, and for his own safety they gave him a new identity – Jonathan Naylor – and moved him to Northern Ireland, which is where I grew up… in abject poverty.' Martin's colour rose as if the memories were causing him a great deal of anger. 'The authorities were happy to change his and my mother's details, but because I was still a baby, they forgot me, and I grew up as Max. As a young man on the streets of Belfast, I learned how to fight, I learned how to cheat, and I learned that if you want anything in this world, you have to take it. Forged papers were easy to come by and comparatively cheap. When I was twenty, I came to England and did three years of university – under my freshly assumed name of Martin Naylor, the name written on my degree certificate. Although, I assume that after all this, my qualifications will be null and void. I landed my first teaching post in York and that's when it became my hometown.'

There was a considerable pause while he drank from a cup of water and gathered his thoughts. Watching through the two-way glass, Joe could not help but be impressed by Gemma's patience, and that of the chief inspector. Everyone knew that Roy Vickers was not the most tolerant man in the West Yorkshire division, and for his part, Joe was already anxious to get through the tale. Had he been in the interview room, he would have been badgering Martin to get on with the story.

'I married virtually straight from university, and as you're aware, my first wife passed away. And she did die of natural causes, by the way. It was nothing to do with me. But I came into a considerable sum of money from her insurers. Enough to afford a high quality, forged passport and birth certificate. After the funeral, after selling the house, and tidying up all the loose ends, I took off on an extended holiday to the Dordogne, which is where I met Francine. I brought her back to England, moved up to Darlington, and as you know, we were married – as Mr and Mrs Nellis.' He laughed cynically at the memory. 'Dear God, she was expensive. You can talk all you like about high maintenance; it didn't come any higher than Frankie. Fights were regular, and it wasn't long before the neighbours began to complain. And then, somewhere along the line, I remembered the money I'd come into after Gillian's death. I had Frankie insured for fifty thousand, and it wouldn't be too great a problem to be rid of her. Odds and sods of household chemicals mixed into her food and drink, just to give her a history of gastric problems, and then a final dose of something strong enough to kill her. I'd be rid of a liability and so much wealthier for it.'

'But you didn't go through with it,' Vickers observed.

Martin chuckled. 'I never got the chance. She must have tumbled what I was doing, and she disappeared. To be honest, I was as puzzled as everyone else. Not by her disappearance, obviously, but I couldn't find her. Family, friends, relatives, most of them in France of course, hadn't heard from her. My biggest fear was that she'd gone to the police, but gradually, as time went by and they never took any serious interest in me, I began to relax. But even after seven years, I could not find her, so I had her formally declared dead, and I collected fifty grand.' He laughed aloud this time. 'We even had a mock funeral for her. What a farce. An empty box containing a framed photograph of her. As far as I know, it's still there, buried in Darlington's main cemetery.'

In an effort to stick to the tale, Gemma said, 'Your neighbours' tongues never stopped wagging though, did they?'

Martin frowned. 'Vicious and spiteful. That's what they were. And there was no justification for it. All right, so I made her throw up a few times, but I didn't kill her… as you know… as we all know now. It was largely thanks to them that I left Darlington and moved to Ripon, which is where I met Deirdre, and I know you won't believe me, but at the time, I knew nothing of Billy Trelfus. He only became a problem much later. By now, I'd changed my identity again. I was Marlon Newman. Expensive getting the necessary documentation, but I had money in the bank then, and Deirdre had a sweet little house worth almost a quarter of a million, although there was only a hundred and fifty thousand in equity. I made no mistake this time. Deirdre suffered from brachycardia; an unusually slow heartbeat, and she took atropine to correct it. Substituting a harmless gel for her medication brought on the first heart attack. And when she died within a couple of weeks – overdose of her drugs, this time – there was no requirement for a post-mortem. Even the police thought I'd suffered enough, and by the time they exhumed the body a couple of years later, and learned that the second heart attack had been induced, it was too late. Marlon Newman had sold the house, taken the money, taken the insurance, and disappeared, and I was Martin Naylor once again.'

Vickers waited for Gemma to finish making notes, and then asked, 'So what brought you to Sanford?'

Martin shrugged. 'A combination of factors. I'd read of the old boy claiming the woman who murdered his daughter in Ripon was living here. Billy Trelfus actually made the national tabloids with his idiotic claim. But if he was serious, he could only be one talking about one woman: Francine. Naturally, he didn't know she was innocent, but if she was indeed in Sanford, I had to find her and shut her up… permanently. Beyond that, I was running out of money again. You'd never believe how fast I can spend it. Not on flashy cars or large houses, but on simple things like long holidays in the Bahamas and the Seychelles. Like it or not, I had to go back to work, and Sanford Park Comprehensive were looking for a suitably qualified English teacher. I applied, I was selected. It was a good move. You Yorkshire folk are all thickheads essentially. You've never been educated beyond the very basic, and why should you be? If we boil it all down, you're all miners and foundry workers. You don't need education. Wriggling my way through the predictable questions of an appointments panel was child's play to me. I'd done it so many times before.'

'But you didn't kill Billy right away?'

'I couldn't. I needed to shut him up, true, but I was hoping he'd lead me to Frankie first. It goes without saying that he never did. He never left the house other than to go to the shop or the pub, and he was barred from a lot of them.'

'And in the meantime, you homed in on Sheila?'

'She was a tough proposition,' Martin said. 'Not quite as singular and virginal as she made out, but certainly not a pushover like her friend Jump.'

On hearing this slight against Brenda's fun-loving nature, Joe almost went ballistic, but Don Oughton urged him to calm down and keep quiet. His anger bubbling away, Joe wondered if Martin and Brenda had… He cut the thought off and continued listening.

On the other side of the glass, Martin went on, 'Like most women in this town, Sheila's a habitual gossip, with a tendency to brag about what she has. Two fine sons, both conveniently living in America, a house valued at a hundred and eighty thousand or more, the mortgage paid off, and of course, she was insured to the hilt. A quarter of a million.'

'But her sons were the beneficiaries,' Vickers pointed out.

Martin looked vaguely irritated. 'Yes, that was a bit of an eye-opener. I planned to contest it when everything was over and done with. The kids would have got something, sure, but I'm certain I could have persuaded the courts to let me have the bulk of it.'

In the observation room, Joe sat fuming. He longed to reach through the glass, wrap his hands around Martin's throat, and squeeze the life out of him. He'd been ready to murder Sheila, rob those two boys of their rightful inheritance, and his devil may care attitude to the interrogation, perfectly in tune with Joe's 1950s ideas of Russian coldness, showed no hint of remorse.

Back in the interview room, the police had moved on. 'Sheila fell ill during your honeymoon,' Gemma pointed out. 'Was that you?'

'Of course it was. She has a cast-iron stomach. I simply added one or two drops of household chemicals – washing-up liquid, disinfectant, bleach – to her meals.' He laughed. 'All her meals. Not enough for her to notice, but enough to churn her stomach. And it was only natural for her to blame the foreign food. She's a Yorkshirewoman, isn't she? If it isn't cooked in three inches of lard, she doesn't believe it's edible.'

Both officers were becoming irritated with his demeaning attitude towards their fellow Yorkists.

'And the holly tree?' Vickers demanded.

'A simple enough job when we got back from Cape Verde and she was laid up with her gastric problems. I took all the berries from the existing tree so I could use them to screw up her gut again, and I spent one night, the whole bloody night, digging it out and putting a new one in its place. It was bloody hard work, but necessary. I knew she'd call on that know-it-all so-and-so, Robson, and he would tell her that the bush was too young to produce berries, and Sheila being Sheila, she would tell him how wrong he was. It was vital, you see. If any of the tests her GP, that damn fool Khalil, ordered should come back with traces of saponin, I had to be sure that they couldn't track it down to the garden. I eventually told her of the switch when I'd heard that Robson had been to see Murray.' A broad grin spread across his face. 'You don't know how much I enjoyed watching Murray and Jump playing burglars in the back garden. They don't need anyone to make fools of them. They manage perfectly well on their own.'

By now it was obvious that Gemma was struggling to control her anger. 'And the bleach? A bit harsh wasn't it?'

'The amount of crap I've been feeding her since September, I knew it would be enough.' He laughed again. 'God, if only she knew what a bloody fool I'd been making of her.'

'Joe Murray had the last laugh, though, didn't he?' Gemma challenged.

Martin sucked in his breath. 'Murray's a pain. I can't argue with his observational abilities, and you have to admire his guts, but basically, he had nothing. Not until he turned up Frankie.'

Vickers consulted Gemma's notes. 'Which brings us nicely back to Billy Trelfus.'

Martin shrugged. 'It was that rumour from years before. I couldn't let it go. Even though he never led me to Frankie, it was still too much of a coincidence for my liking, Deirdre had photograph albums, you know, and the moment I clapped eyes on him, I knew he was her father. God knows what he was doing in Sanford.'

'He'd been here since just after the war,' Gemma said, demonstrating that the police had looked into Trelfus's history. 'He came here for the work.'

'I wasn't that interested in his history. I just knew I'd have to get rid of him eventually, especially as I'd begun to work on Sheila. Think about it. Even if you didn't suspect me of killing Sheila, Murray would plaster my name all the local papers, and if Frankie saw it – assuming she really was in Sanford – it would open up the enquiry we're involved in right now. The very enquiry I've made every effort to avoid. So I bided my time, and my chance came that night. I'd been watching his house for a while, and when I saw that builder, drunk, completely plastered, go into the house next door with his girlfriend, I knew the time was right. About half an hour later, the girlfriend's mother turned up.' He frowned. 'I'm surprised I didn't recognise Frankie, but then, she is a good few years older, and she's put some weight on. Anyway, when they left, I knocked on Trelfus's back door. I told him who I was and how I was looking for Frankie too, and he practically dragged me inside. There was a bit of an argument, but he was like that, you know. A lot like Deirdre. Cantankerous. When I told him that Frankie was innocent, and that I'd murdered Deirdre, he picked up a walking stick and came at me.' Martin smiled across the table. 'You see what I mean about you

Yorkshire thickies? If he'd had any intelligence, he would have guessed that the only reason I told him was because I was going to kill him.'

Vickers sighed. 'Just get on with the tale, Mr Naylor.'

'My timing was absolutely perfect. He came at me waving his walking stick, I hooked my foot behind his, gave him a push and he fell back, hit his head on the table or something. A quick check on his pulse to make sure he was fading, and that was good enough for me. If rattling his head like that hadn't killed him, I'd have finished the job anyway. And when I read that you had arrested that idiot builder from next door, I could hardly believe my luck.' Martin yawned.

The police had all they needed, and Gemma finally put down her pen and glowered at him. 'You have absolutely no remorse, do you? Murder, attempted murder, perverting the course of justice, false identities, and you don't give a toss.'

'This is a dog eat dog world, Inspector, and all my life, I've been the bigger dog. I did what I had to do to make my way in the world.'

'All the way to a life sentence,' Vickers concluded.

Martin chuckled gleefully. 'Diminished responsibility, I'll be hospitalised, and they'll let me out one day. And if he's still around, Murray had better watch his step. And Sheila Riley, and Brenda Jump…' He smiled at Gemma. 'And you.'

* * *

It was gone six o'clock when Joe got back to the hospital, to find Sheila out of bed, packing her bags, a doctor arguing with her, and Brenda standing helplessly by.

'What's the problem?' Joe demanded.

'Sheila's discharging herself,' Brenda explained.

The doctor turned appealing eyes on Joe. 'Mrs Naylor is not yet—'

Sheila cut him off. 'I've told you before, my name is Riley. I do not want to hear that awful name again. Not in connection with me, I don't. And now that the cause of my problems has been ascertained, and the miscreant put away – hopefully for the rest of his life – I shall be back to normal in no time. In case you've all forgotten, it's Christmas tomorrow, and I have no intentions of spending it in hospital. I'll be better off at home.' She gave the doctor a look of Amazonian determination. A look Joe and Brenda knew well. A look which brooked no argument. 'Now would you kindly arrange for my prescriptions so I can get out of here?'

The doctor made one last appeal. 'Obviously, I can't stop you—'

'That's right. You can't.'

The medic pressed on regardless. 'Your prescriptions may not be enough, Mrs Naylor... Riley. You still need care.'

Joe nudged Brenda who realised at once what the silent hint meant. 'The doctor's right, Sheila. As a compromise, why not stay with me? I have room, and I can keep an eye on you. Make sure everything is as it should be.'

Sheila's irritation settled on her best friend. 'Brenda—'

This time Joe interrupted her. 'You've been telling us to use our heads for the last fifty years. Why don't you listen to your own advice, Sheila? You need someone to look after you. Martin is no longer part of this equation, and when it comes to looking after people, I'm as much use as a chocolate teapot. Brenda is perfect for the job.'

'But The Lazy Luncheonette?'

'I can bring people in to fill the gaps. Besides, you may be right as a bobbin by the New Year. Now use your head. Go to Brenda's.'

Sheila gave the matter a little consideration, and eventually nodded, much to the doctor's relief. 'I'll arrange for your prescriptions and the discharge papers.'

He left, and Sheila sat on the bed, her eyes on Joe. 'The police station?'

He drew in a deep breath. 'I'm sorry, Sheila. Martin has admitted everything. He tried to kill Frankie all those years ago, but she escaped, he definitely murdered Deirdre Ullsworth, and he also killed Billy Trelfus. If we hadn't got here in time, you'd have been his next victim.'

Her slim features fell, and she suddenly looked years older. She turned an uncharacteristically self-pitying face on her two friends. 'And I treated you two so badly. I even tried to get you thrown out of the 3rd Age Club. I… I really don't know what to say.'

Brenda forced a smile of encouragement.

'Then don't say anything. Just come with us back to my place, and we'll enjoy Christmas as best we can, all three of us.'

Chapter Nineteen

On Wednesday morning, along with the rest of the UK, bells rang out and the world awoke to another Christmas Day. In Sanford, the familiar family holiday brought more icy rain and slippery pavements, but no trace of the White Christmas promised by sensationalist tabloid headlines.

Joe traditionally passed the morning on the phone to friends and family, and the afternoons in the company of Lee, Cheryl and young Danny. The events of the previous few days called for a change. His early routine remained the same. He rang friends and family alike, and exchanged season's greetings with them.

Les Tanner had a little more to say than "Merry Christmas". 'Following on from Monday evening and Naylor's full confession yesterday, I think the whole of the 3rd Age Club owes you and Brenda an apology. I'm due back at the town hall on Monday, but between now and then, I'll issue a statement to the membership, formally apologising and rescinding the censure motion. And I do hope you will keep up your campaign to replace me in the Chair by the end of next month.'

Joe had many reasons to be critical of Les, but when it came to the nitty-gritty of committee procedure, he could not be faulted. 'I'll leave it to you to tell Stewart Dalmer. It'll just about ruin his Christmas. Enjoy your few days off, Les, and I'll see you at the next club meeting.'

With the phone calls completed, he visited Lee and his wife and son in the morning, left presents for them, and passed an hour in their company, after which he drove to Brenda's where he would spend the rest of the day with her and a naturally downhearted Sheila.

When he arrived, Brenda led him into the kitchen. 'Sheila's on Zoom to her sons. Bringing them up to speed. She keeps breaking down crying.'

'Understandable, given the circumstances. The shock's beginning to set in.'

With her permission, he moved to the open back door, and lit a cigarette, and from there he gave her a rundown of his conversation with Les Tanner. Brenda applauded their chairman's decision, and Joe concluded by asking after Sheila's health and state of mind.

'Bad. We haven't had a great deal of sleep. Her stomach is still a bit of a mess, and I can only imagine that it'll take a while for things to settle properly. The prescriptions help, and she had it right when she said she was better out of hospital. If we'd left her there, she would have done nothing but brood on the way things have turned out.' Brenda, so often the life and soul of any party, did not look as if she was in a celebratory mood. 'I'll be glad when all this is behind us.'

'We're talking a good few months, I should think. Still, according to Gemma, he'll get what he deserves. The rest of his life in a cell.'

'But didn't you say he was going to plead diminished responsibility?'

'He won't get away with it. All those chemicals he used? He's as sane as me and you..'

Brenda sighed. 'And what about poor old Billy Trelfus?'

'A miserable old git. A snapper, but he didn't deserve to die like that.' Joe grinned. 'I'm talking as a professional gripe.'

'If Bailey hadn't been so drunk that night, he might have heard the argument and collared Naylor.'

'That's what I mean about him being sane. He had everything planned.' Joe took another drag on his cigarette. 'There's nothing to be gained from what ifs and might-have-beens, Brenda. Let's just be thankful we saved Sheila.'

Brenda nodded, and passed him a small glass of sherry. Sitting at the far end of the table where she could speak to him without raising her voice, she asked, 'How are we going to pull her through, Joe?'

He sipped at the wine and pulled a face. 'Give me a pint of Guinness anytime.' Putting the glass on the table, he stubbed out his cigarette in the sink, and sat with Brenda, screwing up his face in a passable impression of deep thought. 'We're friends. Isn't that what friends are for? To help you through the worst times? Anyway, I have had an idea. It came to me last night while I was emailing Alison.'

Brenda chuckled but it was without humour. 'You were emailing Alison? You're still carrying a torch for her, aren't you?'

'Yes, but my batteries are not too good.

Anyway, I owe her after that business in Palmanova.'

'Your idea?'

'Simple,' Joe admitted. 'I got the idea from Archie Hepple the other day. He's going to Lanzarote, early in the New Year. How about we float off to Tenerife for a week? Say Easter time? Just us three. It'll give Sheila the chance to recover properly, and it'll help brighten her up. All that sunshine, and there's plenty of good entertainment, sixties and seventies music like what we like. And don't worry if you're a bit strapped for cash. The Lazy Luncheonette will pay for it.'

'Out of our profit share?' Brenda giggled again and fell silent, contemplating the proposition. 'It's a good idea, Joe, but I think it would be better if we put it to the club, as a proper holiday option. You'd get a better price from the hotel, and aside from that, if it's just us three, it might grate on Sheila's nerves; remind her too much of all this. With the rest of the club there – as many of them who can afford it – we can have a proper party.'

'All right, then. I'll bring it up at the meeting in January. You know. The one where I'll be re-elected chairman.'

'You hope.'

'I *know*.'

They were interrupted by Sheila's entry into the kitchen. She greeted Joe with a thin and weary smile.

'Peter and Aaron?' he asked.

'Concerned, but relieved that everything

turned out well. They send their regards to you both… and their thanks, of course. And also their apologies for the nasty email they sent you.'

'I've already binned it,' Joe lied. 'No damage done.' As he used the word "damage" Joe suddenly realised that Sheila might put a different interpretation on it, and he hastened on to qualify his statement. 'Not to me, anyway.'

Brenda offered her the sherry bottle and she refused. 'A cup of tea, perhaps. Weak, with no milk'

Her best friend nodded and moved to the kettle. Soon, when they were seated again, Joe tried to open the conversation.

'We were just saying—'

Sheila cut him off. 'No. Let me speak, Joe.' The muscles of her slim face worked agitatedly in an effort to control her emotions. 'You tried to tell me and I wouldn't listen.'

'You loved him, Sheila,' Brenda excused her. 'We're all the same. When someone attacks those we love, we defend them to hell and back. Neither I nor Joe hold it against you.'

'And if it's any consolation,' Joe said, 'we're seriously sorry that things turned out this way. You know how much I like to be right, but this time I'd give my eye teeth to be wrong.'

'I know. It'll take me some time to get over this. Maybe I'll never get over it. Maybe I will never trust any man ever again.' She smiled at Joe. 'Present company excepted. I said on the day Martin and I married, that the one thing which would never change is my love for you two, but it very nearly did fail. I hurt you both. Badly. And for that I am so very, very sorry. I owe a huge debt of gratitude to you. I didn't listen and it could have cost me my life. I don't know how I'll ever repay you.'

Tears began to trickle down her cheek. Joe turned away. Women who cried always made him feel guilty… even when he had nothing to feel guilty about.

Brenda, also on the verge of tears, took Sheila's hand. 'We can never put a price on friendship, and it never incurs debts. We may be sad, disappointed at the way things turned out for you, and it's put a damper on a time of year that we've always enjoyed, but we're overjoyed that you're still with us. Aren't we, Joe?'

'Can't argue with that.'

'You owe us nothing,' Brenda declared..

Joe grinned. 'Well, maybe a pint when we get to Tenerife.'

The women dissolved into tearful laughter, and when it trailed off, Sheila cast him a quizzical glance. 'Tenerife?'

Brenda nodded at their friend and employer. 'Mastermind's idea. A week in the Canary Islands sometime around Easter. He thinks the sunshine and free-flowing drink will do us all the power of good.'

Sheila tried to smile again. 'Don't let anyone tell you that you don't have the best ideas, Joe.'

He beamed broadly at them. 'In that case, I'll get onto the travel agent tomorrow morning.'

'It's Boxing Day, Joe/. They'll be shut.'

'The day after then.' He raised his glass. 'In the meantime, here's to a Merry Christmas.'

THE END

THANK YOU FOR READING. I HOPE YOU HAVE ENJOYED THIS BOOK. WOULD YOU BE KIND ENOUGH TO LEAVE A RATING OR REVIEW ON AMAZON?

The Author

David W Robinson retired from the rat race after the other rats objected to his participation, and he now lives with his long-suffering wife in sight of the Pennine Moors outside Manchester.

Best known as the creator of the light-hearted and ever-popular **Sanford 3rd Age Club Mysteries**, **Mrs Capper's Casebooks** and in a similar vein the Spookies Paranormal Mysteries. He also produces darker, more psychological crime thrillers as in the **Feyer & Drake** thrillers and occasional standalone titles sometimes under the pen name **Robert Devine**

He, produces his own videos, and can frequently be heard grumbling against the world on Facebook at https://www.facebook.com/davidrobinsonwriter/ and has a YouTube channel at https://www.youtube.com/user/Dwrob96/videos. For more information you can track him down at www.dwrob.com and if you want to sign up to my newsletter and pick up a #FREE book or two, you can find all the details at https://dwrob.com/readers-club/

By the same Author

The Sanford 3rd Age Club Mysteries

A decade on from their debut, there are 26 volumes and a special in the Sanford 3rd Age Club Mystery series.

We follow the travels and trials of amateur sleuth Joe Murray and his two best friends, Sheila Riley and Brenda Jump. The short, irascible Joe, proprietor of The Lazy Luncheonette in Sanford, West Yorkshire, jollied along by the bubbly Brenda and Sheila, but only his friends, but also his employees, all three leading lights in the Sanford 3rd Age Club (STAC for short). And it seems that wherever they go on their outings on holidays in the company of the born-again teenagers of the 3rd Age Club, they bump into… MURDER.

A major series of whodunits marinated in Yorkshire humour, they are exclusive to Amazon and free to read for subscribers to Kindle Unlimited. The publisher, Darkstroke Books will close later this year and the publishing rights are reverting in blocks of five. You can find the newer editions at: https://mybook.to/stacser and if you wish to read those still attributed to Darkstroke Books, you can find them at: https://mybook.to/stacser

Mrs Capper's Casebooks

Christine Capper is a solid, down to earth Yorkshire lass, witty, plain spoken, but with an innate sense of inquiry (all right, then, she's nosy). She passes her days in the West Yorkshire town of Haxford looking after her long-suffering husband, Dennis, a man with an obsession for all things automotive, and putting him right when he goes wrong, which is more often than not. She takes care of their pet, Cappy the Cat, a feline with attitude, dotes on her granddaughter Bethany, and is openly proud of her son, Simon, now Acting Detective Constable Capper of the Haxford force.

A former police officer, she's Haxford's only trained and licenced private investigator. She's choosy about the cases she takes on but appears destined to be dragged into more serious affairs, during which she passes on her findings to her friend, Detective Sergeant Mandy Hiscoe and Mandy's immediate boss, DI Paddy Quinn, a man who is quite open about his dislike for private eyes.

A series of light-hearted mysteries, laced with Yorkshire grit and wit, Mrs Capper's Casebooks are exclusive to Amazon available for the Kindle and in paperback.

You can find them at:
https://mybook.to/cappseries

The Spookies Paranormal Mysteries

The misadventures of Lady Concepta (aka Sceptre)Rand-Epping and her two ghost-hunting partners, private eye Pete Brennan and ducker and diver, Kevin Keeley, not forgetting Sceptre's ghostly butler, Fishwick as they tackle bad guys from this world and the Other Side.

A series of light-hearted ghost hunts mingled with more earthly crimes. Learn more at:
https://dwrob.com/spookies/

Other Works

I also turn out darker works such as The Anagramist and The Frame with Chief Inspector Samantha Feyer and civilian consultant Wesley Drake.

The Feyer & Drake series are published Bloodhound books. For more information visit https://www.bloodhoundbooks.com/

Printed in Great Britain
by Amazon

STAGE FRIGHT

Contents

Scaredy Cat   3
The Vanishing Box   27

WRITTEN BY ADAM AND CHARLOTTE GUILLAIN
ILLUSTRATED BY AMERIGO PINELLI

Published by Pearson Education Limited, Edinburgh Gate, Harlow, Essex, CM20 2JE
Registered company number: 872828

www.pearsonschools.co.uk

Text © Adam and Charlotte Guillain 2011

Designed by Bigtop
Original illustrations © Pearson Education 2011
Illustrated by Amerigo Pinelli

The right of Adam and Charlotte Guillain to be identified as authors of this work has been asserted by them in accordance with the Copyright, Designs and Patents Act 1988.

First published 2011

15 14 13 12
10 9 8 7 6 5 4 3

British Library Cataloguing in Publication Data
A catalogue record for this book is available from the British Library

ISBN 978 1 408 27402 6

Copyright notice
All rights reserved. No part of this publication may be reproduced in any form or by any means (including photocopying or storing it in any medium by electronic means and whether or not transiently or incidentally to some other use of this publication) without the written permission of the copyright owner, except in accordance with the provisions of the Copyright, Designs and Patents Act 1988 or under the terms of a licence issued by the Copyright Licensing Agency, Saffron House, 6–10 Kirby Street, London EC1N 8TS (www.cla.co.uk). Applications for the copyright owner's written permission should be addressed to the publisher.

Printed and bound in Malaysia, CTP-PJB

Acknowledgements
We would like to thank the children and teachers of Bangor Central Integrated Primary School, NI; Bishop Henderson C of E Primary School, Somerset; Brookside Community Primary School, Somerset; Cheddington Combined School, Buckinghamshire; Cofton Primary School, Birmingham; Dair House Independent School, Buckinghamshire; Deal Parochial School, Kent; Newbold Riverside Primary School, Rugby and Windmill Primary School, Oxford for their invaluable help in the development and trialling of the Bug Club resources.

Every effort has been made to contact copyright holders of material reproduced in this book. Any omissions will be rectified in subsequent printings if notice is given to the publishers.

Scaredy Cat

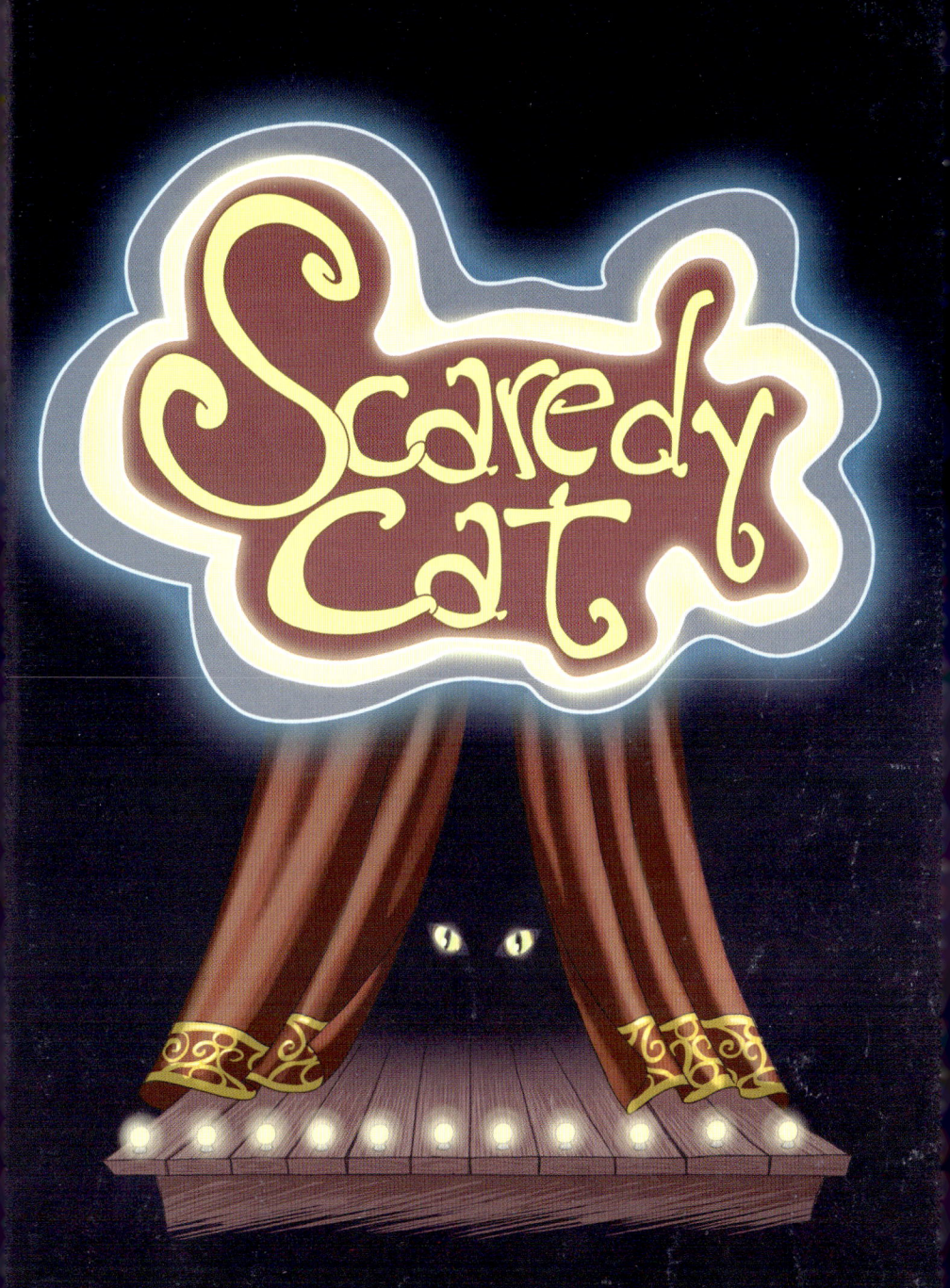

It was Saturday afternoon and Zak and Zoe Brightly were walking to the theatre at the end of the pier. The theatre was important to their family. Mrs Brightly was the director. She planned the shows. Mr Brightly worked backstage, making the sets.

5

"Mum says Dan James has got the starring role in this summer's show," said Zak.

"*The* Dan James!" gasped Zoe. "The Dan James who won the talent show on TV?"

"Yes," said Zak. "Dad says he'll be at the rehearsal today."

"Come on then," said Zoe, starting to run. "I don't want to miss this!"

"I'll race you," said Zak, looking at the darkening sky. A storm was brewing.

The children ran into the theatre just as the rain started to fall. All the seats were empty so Zak and Zoe sat in the front row.

"Wow, Dan is brilliant," said Zoe after the rehearsal.

"He is," agreed Zak. "I hope we can meet him later."

Mrs Brightly went onto the stage and began talking to the actors.

"This is going to take ages," said Zoe. "Let's play hide and seek."

Zak and Zoe loved playing in the theatre when it was closed to the public. It was a bit spooky, but there were lots of places to explore.

As well as the stage, there were all the dressing rooms where the actors got ready, the workshop where the sets were made, the orchestra pit, and the control booth for the lights and sound.

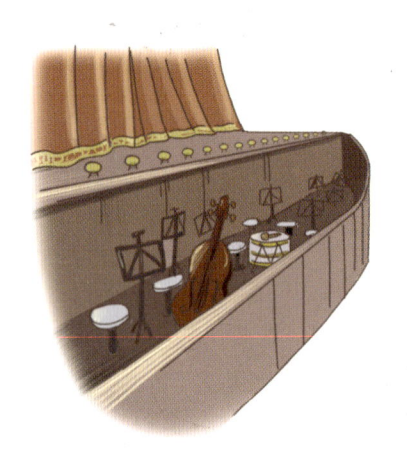

But there was one place where Zak and Zoe Brightly were not allowed to go.

"You must never, *ever* go under the stage," the children were warned.

"It's dark and packed with old props, and it's very dangerous."

When they were bored with playing hide and seek, Zak and Zoe went to find Mrs Brightly. She was still busy with the actors. Zak turned to his sister. There was a gleam in his eye.

"Let's look under the stage," he whispered. "I want to see what it's like down there."

"But we're not allowed!" Zoe gasped. "If we get caught we'll be in BIG trouble."

"Well, we won't get caught then," said Zak. "I want to find the trap door that Dan James uses in the show. Come on."

Zak led Zoe down some steps to an old wooden door behind the stage.

"But Mum and Dad said ..." Zoe hesitated.
"Scaredy cat," Zak teased.
Zoe shook her head and turned away.
"What's the matter?" sneered Zak. "Cat got your tongue?"
"He will," said a spooky voice, "if you're foolish enough to go down there."
The children froze.
"Who said that?" Zoe whispered.
The voice seemed to be coming from behind the door.

Suddenly, the door flew open and out burst Dan James.

The children jumped in fright.

"You called your sister a 'scaredy cat'," said Dan, turning to Zak. "That wasn't very nice. Do you know the story of the Scaredy Cat?"

Zak shook his head.

"The legend of the Scaredy Cat is no joke," Dan went on, lowering his voice. "The Scaredy Cat lurks in the dark corners of theatres. He preys on foolish children who don't listen to warnings."

Dan looked back and peered into the shadows, as if the Scaredy Cat might be lurking there. "Whenever you hear someone ask, 'Cat got your tongue?' you can be sure the Scaredy Cat is close by," Dan warned. "And that's exactly what will happen to you if the Scaredy Cat catches you messing about under the stage. You'll scream but no sound will come out."

Zak and Zoe gasped.

"You mean he'll take your tongue?" whispered Zoe.

"He'll take your entire voice," said Dan. "There'll be no crying out for help if the Scaredy Cat gets you. So listen to your parents and don't play down there. It's dark and very dangerous."

With that, Dan James made a dramatic exit.

Zak turned to his sister. "That's rubbish!" he scoffed. "I'm going to explore. Are you coming?"

Zoe shook her head.

"You really are a scaredy cat!" laughed Zak.

Zak opened the forbidden door. A rush of stale air, as cold as a ghost, swept over him. He shivered. Something ran over his foot, but it was gone before he could see what it was.

The hairs at the back of his neck bristled. As he started to walk down the creaking steps, the door behind him swung closed, leaving Zak in the murky gloom.

A rotten smell wafted by him. Zak squirmed, feeling a bit sick.

He could hear the waves pounding against the legs of the pier below him. The wind was battering the theatre above.

A single bulb in the middle of the ceiling cast a dim light. Zak carefully made his way through the junk and shadows. "This place is nothing but a dumping ground for old props," he muttered.

Old models stood among rails of costumes. A golden throne was stacked on top of a king's chariot. Zak was about to climb into the time-machine that his dad had made for the last pantomime ... when the light went out!

Darkness flooded the room. "The storm must have cut the power," thought Zak. "Time to get out of here!"

He fumbled his way back to where he thought the door was but he stumbled and crashed into things. Turning this way and that, he soon had no idea where the door was.

"Help!" he shouted. "Someone help me!" His voice was lost against a crash of thunder outside.

Zak felt panic rising. Something moved in his hair. His hands flapped wildly to knock it out.

"It's just cobwebs," he told himself, shuddering at the thought of the huge spiders that might be creeping around him.

Suddenly there was a crash, followed by a rattling sound that echoed around the room like a slowly fading alarm bell.

"It's just an old bucket or something," Zak told himself, trying to be brave.

Then the room fell deathly silent. The storm had passed. All Zak could hear now was the pounding of his heart. He took some deep breaths. His eyes scanned the darkness.

"There's something in here," he thought. "I can feel it." His mind shot to the Scaredy Cat. Suddenly there was a loud squeal and Zak jumped with fright.

Zak bolted, crashing through anything that stood in his way.

Loud, terrifying screeches pierced the darkness. Zak stumbled against a pillar, then felt a sharp pain in his ankle.

"Get off me!" he yelled. He imagined the Scaredy Cat's claws sinking deep into his skin. Zak's imagination raced. Pictures flashed into his mind. "How big can this Scaredy Cat be?" he gasped.

Just then he ran into a wall.

"Ow!" he cried, clutching at his throbbing nose, but he couldn't stop. Something was coming towards him. Zak dodged to one side, but hit another wall. "Oh no! I'm cornered," he thought.

Zak turned around to face whatever it was that was coming towards him. Two fiery eyes glared out of the darkness. Then he saw it: a huge black cat with bared claws.

The Scaredy Cat was coming to rip out his tongue!

He slammed his eyes shut and tried to scream but NOTHING came out …

It was the longest silent scream Zak Brightly could ever have imagined. When there was no air left in his lungs, he collapsed against the wall and gasped for breath.

"Zak, are you in there?"

It was his dad's voice.

"Zak, where are you?"

Zak opened his eyes. Light was spilling in from the doorway at the end of the room.

"Over here, Dad," Zak tried to shout, but his throat was dry and his voice was sucked away by the air.

A few minutes later, Zak Brightly was out in the backstage corridor with his family.

"How many times have we told you not to play down there?" asked his dad.

Zak opened his mouth but no words came out. He was shaking. "Have I really lost my voice?" he thought.

"Well, at least you're safe now," said Mum, wiping the blood off his face. Zak was black with dirt. His nosebleed had ruined his t-shirt, his trousers were torn and there were cuts on his arms.

"I hear you met Dan James today," said Mum.

"He told us the story of the Scaredy Cat," said Zoe.

"The Scaredy Cat?" asked Dad. "What's that?"

Zoe explained and they laughed.

"Dan's got a cat called Scaredy," said Dad. "He made up that whole spooky story on the spot."

"Come on. Time to go home," said Mum. "I think Zak's had enough excitement for one day."

As the family left the theatre, Zak felt something brush past his legs. He looked back. What was that black shape disappearing into the shadows?

He flinched.

"What's up?" said Zoe. "Cat got your tongue?"

Zak shook his head.

"Then don't ever call me a scaredy cat again," she said.

He never did.

The Vanishing Box

The Pier Theatre
DON'T MISS
MADAM NISHNA
World Famous Illusionist
BE AMAZED

"Can you please hurry up and finish your lunch?" said Mrs Brightly. "We must be at the theatre in time to greet Madam Nishva."

Mrs Brightly was the director of the theatre at the end of the pier.

"Who's Madam Nishva?" asked Zak.

"Madam Nishva is a famous illusionist," said Mr Brightly. "She entertains people with illusions or tricks – like a magician. She performs all over the world. They say the props she uses are amazing!"

"I'd like to take a look at these amazing props," said Zoe.

Mrs Brightly glared at her children.

"You must not touch any of her things," she warned. "Madam Nishva is very strict about that."

Zak and Zoe quickly finished their lunch. They were keen to meet this curious Madam Nishva.

When the Brightlys arrived at the theatre, Madam Nishva was already there.

"Be careful with that!" Madam Nishva shouted at one of the stagehands. "It's my priceless Vanishing Box."

"A priceless Vanishing Box," thought Zoe. "That does sound amazing."

Mrs Brightly greeted Madam Nishva and introduced her family.

"Madam Nishva," said Zoe, politely. "May we come backstage and see some of the props from your show?"

"Absolutely not!" said Madam Nishva. "These things are not toys. They hold dark and mysterious secrets. They could be very dangerous in the wrong hands. Only someone with powers like mine should handle them."

Zak didn't think Madam Nishva looked very powerful. In fact, she looked rather small and thin.

"I have a *very* strong mind," said Madam Nishva, glaring at Zak. Zak looked away. Could she read minds too?

"Do people really vanish inside your Vanishing Box?" Zoe asked.

"Of course," snapped Madam Nishva. "It's extremely powerful, so be warned."

Then Madam Nishva herself seemed to vanish behind a pile of boxes.

"Right then," said Mrs Brightly. "I think the message is loud and clear. Don't go anywhere near that box."

Mr and Mrs Brightly went into the theatre to prepare for the afternoon show.

"Madam Nishva's weird," Zak whispered to his sister.

"She's trying to spook us," said Zoe. "It's just a box."

"Is it?" cried Madam Nishva.

The children jumped. Suddenly, Madam Nishva was standing before them again.

"That Vanishing Box holds secrets beyond your imagination," said Madam Nishva. She lent forward and peered into their eyes. "Come to my show and you will see."

Zak and Zoe loved Madam Nishva's show. There was a glittering hat that seemed to turn rabbits into doves. Then there was a long wooden box which a brave dad from the audience got into. Madam Nishva took out a saw and seemed to cut off his legs and head! The audience gasped, but the man just gave a cheery wave. Everyone was glad to see him walk out of the box at the end of the trick.

The final illusion was the Vanishing Box. Zoe and Zak watched as a nervous boy from the audience stepped inside. Madam Nishva performed a little dance, said some mysterious words and then cried, "SHAZAM!"

When she opened the box, the boy was gone.

"He's hidden inside a secret compartment," Zoe muttered.

"Or there's a trap door under the stage," said Zak.

Madam Nishva turned the open box around. Then she invited people from the audience to come up on stage and look inside it. The boy's mum looked pale. His dad seemed quite pleased. No one could work out what had happened to the boy.

Finally, Madam Nishva did the dance again, cried "SHAZAM!" and the boy appeared in a cloud of smoke.

"What happened?" asked the boy. He looked rather dazed.

"You went to the great city of Marrakesh, in Africa," said Madam Nishva. The boy seemed mesmerized by Madam Nishva's eyes. "You ate jelly and ice-cream in a palace with a beautiful princess. It was amazing!"

"It was amazing!" echoed the boy.

"I want a go inside that box," said Zoe, after the show.

"You'd be wasting your time," said Zak. "It's just a box. You said so yourself."

"But that boy really believed he went to Marrakesh," said Zoe.

When the curtains were drawn and the audience had gone, Zak and Zoe quietly slipped onto the stage. Madam Nishva's props were still there.

"We really shouldn't be here," Zak whispered to his sister. "What if Madam Nishva's stuff really does have dark powers? We could end up anywhere and never get back."

Zoe was just opening the Vanishing Box, when they heard footsteps. They were coming towards the stage.

"Quick!" Zak hissed. "Hide!"

He slid behind some curtains. Zoe froze. Her heart was racing. Then she heard Madam Nishva's voice. She was getting closer. Zoe looked around for a place to hide. There was nowhere except …

Zoe jumped inside the Vanishing Box.

Zak peered through a gap the curtains.

"I heard voices!" shouted Madam Nishva, storming onto the stage. "Who's been meddling with my props?"

Zak's eyes were glued to the Vanishing Box. "Poor Zoe," he thought. "She'll be in real trouble now." He held his breath.

Madam Nishva prowled around the stage.

"I know you're here, somewhere," she muttered. "I can sense your fear."

Madam Nishva brushed her long bony fingers along the wooden box she had sawn through earlier. "Next time, maybe I'll try with a child in here," she chuckled.

Zak gulped. "She's trying to scare us so we give ourselves up," he told himself.

Then Madam Nishva turned to a cage. It was covered with a silk cloth. Slowly, she pulled back the long black cloth. "So, my pretty one," she murmured, "who's been looking at things they shouldn't have?" A red glistening snake hissed and bared its fangs. Its black tongue flickered towards the Vanishing Box.

Zak gasped.

Madam Nishva's eyes shot to the curtain, then straight to the Vanishing Box.

"Ah ha!" she smiled and stepped towards the box.

Just then two stagehands walked onto the stage. Zak sighed with relief.

"The van's waiting at the end of the pier," said one of the men.

He began to load the props into boxes.

"Do be careful," warned Madam Nishva. "These things are very valuable." She turned to the Vanishing Box with a wry smile. "I'll take care of this one."

Zak watched with horror as Madam Nishva reached out to the box …

"What?" thought Zak in astonishment.

He expected Madam Nishva to open the Vanishing Box and find his sister. Instead, she pulled a lever at the back of the box and it started to fold down. But where was Zoe? Soon, the Vanishing Box was completely flat. Madam Nishva packed it into a case.

"Have a nice trip," said Madam Nishva, patting the case. Zak watched in horror. He didn't know what to do. Should he tell Madam Nishva that Zoe had stepped into the box? Was she sending Zoe away?

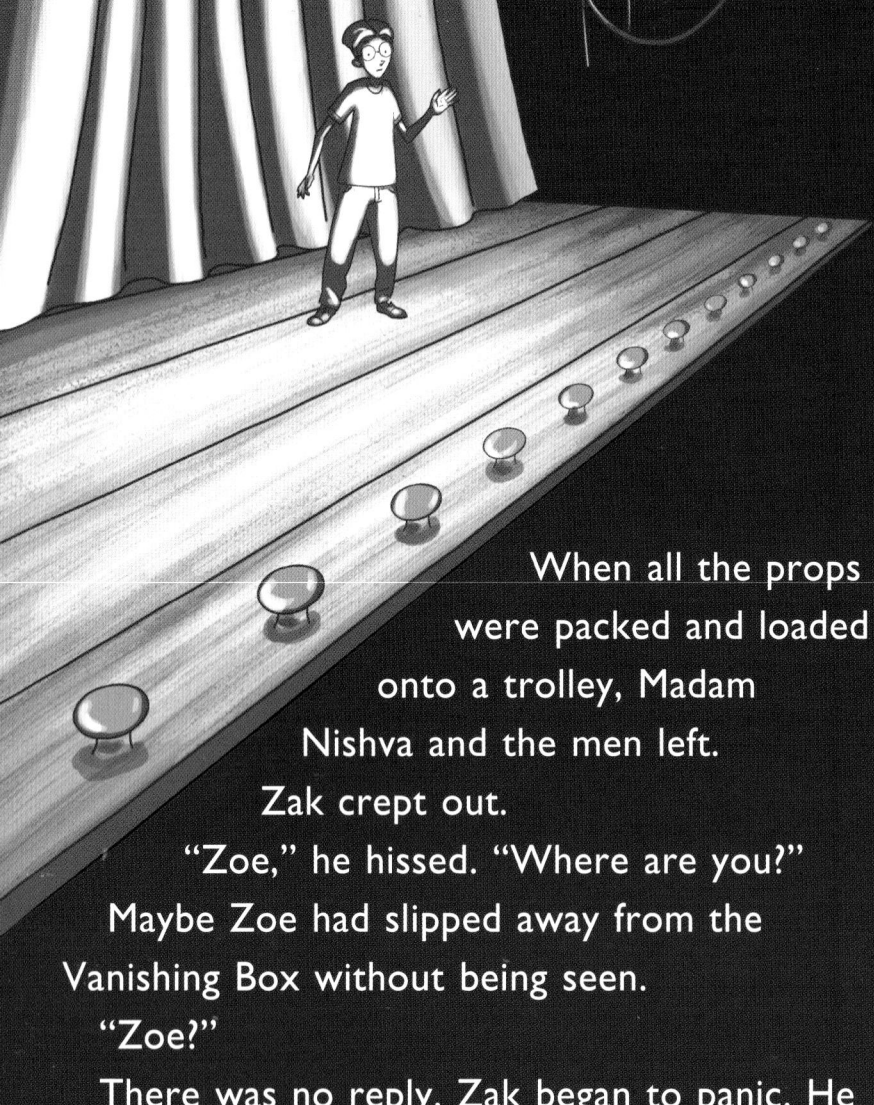

When all the props were packed and loaded onto a trolley, Madam Nishva and the men left.

Zak crept out.

"Zoe," he hissed. "Where are you?"

Maybe Zoe had slipped away from the Vanishing Box without being seen.

"Zoe?"

There was no reply. Zak began to panic. He ran around the theatre. He searched every hiding place he knew, but Zoe was nowhere to be found.

Finally, he ran out onto the pier.

"Oh no," Zak gasped when he saw Madam Nishva's van at the far end of the pier. It was pulling away.

"Stop!" he yelled.

He chased it down the street.

"Stop!" he panted. "Please!"

But no one heard and the van was soon out of sight.

Zak was frantic.

"What if Zoe really has vanished," he thought. "We've got to get her back!"

Zak sprinted back to the theatre. He burst through the doors. His parents were chatting by the box office.

"Zoe's vanished!" he panted. "We need to call the police."

Mr and Mrs Brightly looked startled.

"Quickly," Zak gasped. "She's gone!"

"You're the vanishing one," said Mrs Brightly. "Zoe said she couldn't find you anywhere. She's sitting on the stage right now."

What? Zak was confused. He ran up to the stage and found Zoe looking cross.

"Where have you been?" she asked. "I thought we were going to sneak backstage and discover the secret of Madam Nishva's Vanishing Box."

Zak was baffled.

"You're joking, aren't you?" he said.

"Joking about what?" snapped Zoe.

Zak was speechless.

"Well?" said Zoe.

"We did sneak backstage," Zak told her, "but Madam Nishva surprised us and we had to hide. You jumped inside the Vanishing Box. Don't you remember?"

Zoe looked blank. She shook her head slowly.

"This is too weird for words," thought Zak, collapsing into a seat.

Zak and Zoe sat in silence for a few minutes.

"Perhaps we should let Madam Nishva keep her secrets to herself," said Zoe. "If we knew how the Vanishing Box worked it would spoil the illusion."

Zak looked at Zoe. She seemed a bit different. He hadn't noticed those exotic braids in her hair before.

"Maybe you're right," said Zak.

"Of course I am," said Zoe cheerfully. She jumped down from the stage. "Hey, I'm hungry."

"So am I," said Zak. "Let's buy some doughnuts."

"I know how to make them vanish," said Zoe with a smile.

"Me too," Zak grinned.